Rossi's Cottage

Book 1 in the Moore Love Series

Andrea Kruz & Tabi Lawson

Stone Fruit Press

Copyright © 2025 Andrea Kruz & Tabi Lawson

All rights reserved

The characters and events portrayed in this book are fictitious. Any similarity to real persons, living or dead, is coincidental and not intended by the author.

No part of this book may be reproduced, or stored in a retrieval system, or transmitted in any form or by any means, electronic, mechanical, photocopying, recording, or otherwise, without express written permission of the publisher.

Cover design by: Kip Looney's Art

Stonefruitpress.com

No AI was used in the creation of this book.

To the Austin's of this world who love us through the tragedies, and those who have carried on.

Dear Readers

Thank you for picking up this book and taking a chance on some indie authors. We haven't included a long list of trigger warnings as this book is mostly a clean wholesome small town romance. However in our book, we do touch on pregnancy loss, infertility, grief, medical emergency, severe natural weather events and learning disabilities.

We have tried to address all of these issues with the utmost sensitivity, but we are not experts. We are just two ladies with some lived experience. If you have any concerns reading about these things please put your mental health above all else.

Chapter 1 - Sarah

Charlie said that, except for the name, the Sandbar hadn't changed much over the years, but as I stood looking at it, I hardly recognized the place. I imagine her perspective may be clouded by her proximity to the country kitchen turned bar. The neon signs, at least, were new. I slide my feet back into the shoes I kicked off hours ago and climb out of my Civic, running a hand through my hair, forcing it to behave. Giving up on my thick curls, I straighten my skirt instead.

At the entrance to the Sandbar, I hesitate. I was looking forward to seeing Charlie, but opening this door to the future feels like finally closing the door to my past. Things are over between me and Frank. I have no delusions about that, but this moment feels more final than when I signed the divorce papers. Forcing a smile, I take a deep breath and enter the building.

The Sandbar still smells like greasy fried food, possibly one of the few remaining constants through the years. On my way in, I pass the hen and chick wallpaper, from its time as Sandy's Country Kitchen. When Sandy's switched from chicken to fish and chips, the booths changed to a rustic wood reminiscent of a pirate ship, assuming that the ship sank and the wood was salvaged a few decades later. Corrugated metal littered with expired license plates lines the walls from the building's days as Sandy's Roadhouse. The place seems to be suffering from a bit of an identity crisis.

I chuckle as I walk by the jukebox on my way towards the bar. Charlie spots me first, marking the moment with her patented squeal of delight. Before I can see her, Charlie rounds the bar to wrap me in a hug. We collide mid-stride, where Charlie proceeds to use her few extra inches to lift me to my toes, rocking me back and forth exuberantly. Somewhere in the kitchen, a phone rings.

"It's so good to see you!" she practically yells, stepping back to look me in the eyes.

I laugh. "It's good-"

"Hold that thought." Charlie races away before I finish my practiced response. Her red hair sways from a ponytail as she goes. Snatching an old corded phone off the wall, she answers as professionally as she does everything. "Sandbar. What do you want?... Nope, fresh out." She glances up and waves me closer before resuming her phone conversation. "Alright, fine. If you're gonna make a fuss over it, we'll fix you up. Yup. See you, Austin."

She slams the phone down and yells the order back to the kitchen as I slide onto a barstool. I take a deep breath, attempting to push all the emotions back down where Charlie can't see them. It's a wasted effort, and I attempt a smile.

"Don't go pretending for my benefit," she says, wrinkling her freckles with a smile. She waves a hand at the man a few seats over. "Ignore Duke. He's just here for the free AC. What's rattling around in that head of yours? Do you want to talk about it?"

I glance over and Duke raises his glass to me. "Right. I am just not ready." I paused to clear my throat, to stall. "Maybe we can catch up later?"

Charlie shrugs in some sort of agreement, then changes the subject. "Have you been out to Zia Lena's yet?"

"No, you said if I didn't stop here first, you'd hunt me down. So, here I am." I feel the tears pushing to the surface. All I want is to sit on Zia Lena's couch and cry into her patchouli-smelling shoulder. Inheriting her cottage was so bittersweet. In a way, it was more home to me than the house I shared with Frank. Returning there now, knowing my dear Aunt Lena won't be there to welcome me, feels almost sharper than the pain of starting over at thirty-four.

"Hey," Charlie says, noticing my dip in mood. "None of that. Here." She passes me a caramel coloured beverage.

I push it back across the bar. "I don't think so. I still have errands and things to do."

"Fair enough." Charlie takes a sip and passes the glass to Duke. He raises his new glass to me and polishes it off in an easy gulp. Meanwhile, I try to think of something to say, anything that doesn't dredge up painful memories.

Charlie folds her arms, leaning back on the bar across from me. "So, trivia, Thursdays, seven to nine. You're coming."

"Trivia?" I scoff.

"Yes, trivia," Charlie counters. "What else are you going to do between now and September?"

"I have plenty of work to do at Zia Lena's. Her gardens suffered the most when she got sick." I fidget with my hoop earrings. "Besides, I-"

"Austin!" Charlie shouts over my fumbled attempt to make excuses.

I turn to see a tall, bearded man walk through the door. The sunlight shining in behind him contrasts the dark bar atmosphere, reducing his broad shoulders to an obscure silhouette.

"Stop staring so hard," Charlie says, tapping the bar in front of me. She laughs when I spin around with wide eyes. "Besides, it's not like you don't know him. You remember my brother-in-law. Austin, you remember Sarah, right?"

The man studies me as he saunters closer. "Yeah, hey." He holds a hand out to me. "How's it going?"

His warm hand envelops mine as we shake. He looks familiar, but I can't say that without Charlie mentioning his name, I would have recognized him. But as I study him harder, I suddenly want to remember those kind eyes, and then I recoil at the unwelcome butterflies in my stomach.

"You're Lena's niece, right?" he asks.

I nod. "Yes. You're Noah and William's brother?"

"Unfortunately," he winks as he says it, and a grin forms.

Charlie clicks her tongue, and I realize I've been holding Austin's hand much too long. I let go and turn to face the bar, heat slowly creeping up my face.

Austin clears his throat. "So, Charlie, you got that order ready?"

"I think it'll take a few more minutes. Keep Sarah company while I go check on that." Charlie disappears.

With the sudden urge to chase her down, I wrestle with my nerves. Instead, I force myself to remain sitting as Austin settles on the stool next to me. "Don't mind her. If she's not causing trouble, she's not breathing."

Without looking over at him, I laugh. "So true."

We sit quietly for a moment, and I spot Charlie watching me through the small kitchen window. This is a nightmare. The last thing I want from Osage Beach is to make small talk with a man I barely remember. *What am I going to say? Hi, I'm divorced and childless. How's your happy life going?*

"Are you planning to stay in Osage?" Austin asks.

My mind goes completely blank and I nod. He nods too, looking around the Sandbar.

"That's good," he says encouragingly.

"It is?" I fail to amend my statement to anything socially acceptable.

Austin chuckles. "At the very least, you can keep Charlie out of trouble."

"Right." I nod again as if I don't have an advanced degree and extensive vocabulary, including the basis of the study of morphology. "I, um, took a job at the high school."

His eyes light up. "Oh, yeah? What do you teach?"

"Biology." I look down to see that I have successfully torn a drink napkin into almost equal sections, like confetti. Not wanting to embarrass myself further, I stand. With one foot pointing towards the door, I try for a polite smile. "It was nice catching up with-"

"You're not leaving, are you?" Charlie pouts as she predictably bursts through the kitchen door with a foam container.

"Yeah, I want to unpack tonight, and I'm pretty beat from the drive."

She huffs, holding Austin's lunch captive, and points a finger at me. "You've got my phone number. Call me tonight and we can catch up. And I better see your butt on that stool at least once a week."

Pursing my lips, I nod. "Yup. See you later."

I would agree to just about anything to escape at this particular moment. Safely locked in my Civic, I take a slow breath in until I feel my chest stretch and hold it until I count to three. The air wooshes out of my lungs faster than I can count when I see Austin exit the Sandbar. I find myself watching him walk to his truck.

"Get it together, Sarah," I mumble. Starting the car, I back out and turn left out of the lot.

Chapter 2 - Sarah

I'm trying my damnedest to remain optimistic. So far, it's going so-so. Moving to Osage is my fresh start. Granted, I'm starting way behind where I thought I'd be at this point in my life.

Like it has since the day I signed the papers, the thought pulls my attention to my empty ring finger. I pull into the grocery store, but I only let my gaze sit on my hand for a second before I look back up and square my shoulders. I've made decisions that are right for me and there is no going back. This is my fresh start in my happy place.

To kick off my new life, I plan to dig into Zia Lena's garden this weekend and see what I'm up against to restore it. But first groceries. Groceries, then garden, then who knows. Right, I just have to keep busy.

Busy.

It's a polite euphemism for hiding from my emotions, but the only person who would call me out is Charlie, and she'll be calling me either way. Grabbing my reusable grocery bags, I run through my mental list of needed essentials. This way, I won't have to go out again for a few days.

The Foodland has changed far less than the Sandbar. The fresh produce sits in bins to the right, the pantry items are precariously stacked on shelves to the left and straight ahead is the bakery. For a smalltown grocery store, this place always had the best baked bread. Zia Lena and I used to get a warm Italian loaf when we came in and we'd dip it in olive oil with balsamic vinegar when we got home. Tasty. The familiarity is comforting as I pick out food I don't really like, but I know I should eat.

Years of fertility research have made me an expert on prenatal nutrition. Some days I wonder if it's worth the effort, but I know I want children. I valiantly walk past the Oreos and pick up almonds from the end of the aisle. The occasional splurge is okay, but today I'm in a *finish-the family-sized-box-of-cookies* mood. I don't need the temptation. Leaving the cookie aisle, I head towards the checkout.

The sunshine doesn't quite warm through the cool May air as I leave the store carrying my bags, but we should be safe from freezing temperatures for the growing season. I look forward to digging in the dirt, figuring out where the soil needs amending and raised garden beds need repairing. Zia Lena knew how to care for plants like no one else. I hope being in her garden brings back all the things she taught me. I miss that amazing woman.

She always wore her long, curly salt and pepper hair in a bun, and whether she was digging in the garden or out with friends, those hoop earrings were a part of her outfit. Zia Lena was an Italian spitfire during a time when it was frowned upon for women to be so bold. She was truly one of a kind. Her voice echoes in my memory: *the most important thing for the health of a garden is the gardener, just get your hands dirty*. I plan to do just that.

Still sitting in the driver's seat, feeling the melancholy overtake, I reconsider going back for the cookies. I get so close as to reach for my door handle, but a sign across the road catches my eye.

"A much safer option." I hop out of the car and cross the street.

The bright colours inside Ida's Ice Cream shop lift my spirits. Unsure how much I want to splurge, I take my time perusing the displays.

"Peanut butter-chocolate swirl," a voice interrupts.

My eyes follow the sound to a woman with wispy blond hair, streaked through with white and grey, standing behind the counter. She motions towards a cup of ice cream she's already scooped out of the large bucket.

"Excuse me?" I ask, confused.

"You look like a peanut butter-chocolate swirl to me," she says with a kind smile. "Am I wrong?"

"Oh, I...," Peering into the cup on the counter, I see my favourite ice cream. A generous serving but not too indulgent. "Is this for me?"

She nods and passes me a spoon.

"Have we met before?" I ask just before I tuck a spoonful of the delicious ice cream in my mouth. I have to focus on the woman to hear her over the angel choir singing in my head.

"Not that I can recall right off. You do favour someone I used to know. Oh!" she says with a wider smile. "You're Lena's niece, aren't you?"

"I am. If you didn't remember me, how'd you know I wanted peanut butter-chocolate swirl?" My cup is quickly emptying, and I wonder if I destroy the evidence, would I be able to have seconds.

The blonde woman's eyes dance with a kind of mischief. "You seem like the type of person who knows how to balance the savory simplicity of peanut butter with the rich intensity of chocolate."

I laugh nervously. "I'm not so sure I know how to balance anything these days. This is delicious, though. I'm Sarah," I say, offering to shake with my less sticky left hand.

"Ida." She shakes my hand and passes me a few napkins.

"Thank you." I turn to leave, but remember I haven't paid, or technically ordered, come to think of it. I face Ida again. "How much?" I ask, holding up the cup.

"This one's on me. Welcome back." Ida turns to welcome the teenagers who entered the store just after me.

I only have a few bites left, but I step outside to finish my dessert in private. Ida certainly picked the right flavor. The borderline psychic exchange leaves me uncertain, but I am glad to have met someone who remembers Zia Lena. I plan to visit again as I drop the empty cup in the ice cream cone-shaped trash can.

The drive across town to my new home is short and pleasant enough. The small brick shops selling beach towels and floaties seem much the same, if a little worn. I catch a quick glimpse of the water through the trees and make a mental note to see if my bathing suit fits. The shops turn into farms as I head out of town and drive down the backroad to Zia Lena's cottage. I relish the sight of the orchard, the cottage, the raised gardens, and the spot in the back where we always planned for a greenhouse. That is high on my list, so I can preserve some flowers for propagation through the winter. As I turn down the gravel drive, an ache deep down in my stomach reappears.

Is it Frank? Is it Zia Lena? Is it the missing car seat that should be behind me? Who knows what has triggered this bout of gloominess.

Pulling to a stop in the driveway and turning off the car, I step out of my Civic, fighting the tears. The property looks exactly the same as when I saw it five years ago. Past the small-scale orchard at the front of the homestead sits a tiny but tidy one-story cottage. The front door, as always, is painted a cheery butter yellow. Grey stone pathways lead to the raised bed gardens, fanning out from the cottage and direct you towards the back of the property.

I close the door of my car and there it is, my home away from home. The pressure in my chest which has been growing steadily pushes tears out of my eyes. I can't keep up any longer with swiping them away. Leaving my car, I follow the trail at the front of the house and enter the orchard where I find an apple tree to lean against and cry my heart out.

The melancholy started the minute I pulled away from my rental in Brampton. But after more than two hours driving north, I gave up mourning the life I left behind. Osage Beach always felt more like home to me. Between Zia Lena, Charlie, and some of the Moore brothers, Zach, Noah, and William, I learned more about myself while spending summers on the shore of Georgian Bay than I ever did back in Toronto. That doesn't mean

I'm not heartbroken over the way things ended between me and Frank, but I have to move on. There's no better place to do that than this quiet little town I now call home.

After a few minutes, I calm down, deciding to leave all my tears here. I will not take them inside with me. Our cottage, mine and Zia Lena's, is going to be filled with happiness. Wiping a few tears off my cheek, I sigh deeply and turn to smile at my new home.

Heading to the cottage, I walk up the front steps to the yellow door and put my key in the lock. It's weird to need a key to this place. Despite living alone, Zia Lena never locked the doors, insisting that nothing bad ever happened in this small town. Not that I don't believe in the safety of Osage, but I will be locking my doors.

I walk inside without collecting my bags. The groceries will be okay for a few minutes. I take the time to touch each piece of furniture, the couch by the two large bay windows overlooking my orchard, the dining room table where Charlie will no doubt drink coffee and wine with me, the fireplace where I will set candles and pictures of my family. I let myself feel it all, and then with a deep breath, I force a smile at the future and go to retrieve my bags.

I feel Zia Lena's presence as I unpack my groceries. She's the love in this place. The kitchen is cozy and comfortable with periwinkle cabinets and a white marble countertop.

"If you love yourself and others, you can never go wrong," my bottle of organic cherry juice tells me. Closing my eyes, I absorb that truth. After a slow inhale and exhale, I resume my task. Then, I open the cupboard to find a pair of beady eyes staring me down. The love and the peace are lost as I shriek and slam the cupboard shut. Stuffing my dry goods into the fridge for safekeeping, I grab my keys and head out the door.

Fortunately for me, Osage Beach is a small town, and the hardware store is close by. I pull past Ida's shop, aptly called Ida's Ice Cream Ideations, and make a right into the next parking lot. My eyes glaze over at the landscaping displays that I long to indulge in. This is not the time for that. I need help.

"Mouse traps," I blurt out before the cashier can turn around to greet me. When he does, I feel the heat suddenly rise up my neck and across my cheeks. I know I'm blushing and definitely embarrassed.

Austin Moore gives me one of those half smiles and chuckles. He rubs a hand over his beard and says, "Hello to you too, Sarah. Not happy with your housemates?"

I close my eyes and huff audibly. Fortunately, that is met with more laughter. "Please tell me you have something humane. I don't want to kill it. I just need it to go live somewhere else," I say with a shooing motion.

"I do have catch and release mouse traps, or you could try a glue trap, but then you'd need to peel him out of there to set him free. I can imagine by the look on your face that you wouldn't be too keen on holding hands with the fuzzy creature." Austin steps out from behind the counter and walks me over to the pest control aisle. "Here. This is humane, and you won't see anything. Once he's in here, just take him a ways away from your house and leave the lid open. He'll scurry out."

"Won't he come back?" I ask, staring down at the box.

"Perhaps. It's not as effective as a snap trap or glue trap, but it's humane. If you take them far away, they may stay away, but mice can quickly do damage if left unchecked, so come back if you see any more evidence of the critter," he says with an easy smile.

I take a moment to check the butterflies in my stomach. I assure myself they are due to the mouse, and not those blue eyes that seem to find me so amusing. "Thank you."

"No problem," he tucks his hands in his pockets. "Anything else you need?"

"Not at the moment." I tap the box. "I better get back."

"Sure." Austin walks back to the register with me.

We make small talk for a split second while he rings up my order. The only thing I can think to ask about is his brothers, again. I suddenly remember Austin Moore as the funny older brother. There is another one, a Chris or Connor, I think. He was the serious one. Teenaged Charlie and I mostly spent time with the younger twins, Noah and William, and Zach, of course.

Austin passes me a receipt and smiles. "Stop by anytime, Sarah."

"Thanks," I attempt an easy smile that feels like more of a grimace from where I stand. "I appreciate your help," I add.

"Anytime." Austin turns to help the next customer.

I am grateful for the disruption of the mouse and this subsequent trip to the hardware store, so am a little disappointed when I realize it's time to leave. There's something that has been missing from my life for too long: friendship. That's what I need. *It has nothing to do with Austin's blue eyes*, I tell myself.

I walk out of the store and slide back in my car. Tossing the bag on the passenger seat and turning on the radio, I feel silly for getting worked up over the mouse and Austin. Was he wearing a wedding ring? Is there a Mrs. Austin Moore? And then I ask myself why I care. I drive back to my cottage, armed, a little embarrassed, but excited for my next trip to the hardware store. And not just for the garden stuff.

Chapter 3 - Austin

"No, Mari. Try again," I say, cringing at the mid-drift shirt my eleven-year-old attempts to leave the house in.

Rubbing a hand over my eyes, I miss the eyeroll I know she performed before heading back upstairs. I peek from under my palm at the picture of Jennifer hanging on the wall. Last year, I had two sweet daddy's girls. The closer they get to twelve, the harder this job gets.

"She's turning into you," I mumble at my late wife's picture.

When I lost Jennifer, I didn't think I would survive. A widower in my mid-twenties, responsible for twin baby girls, I only managed with a lot of help from my family. I love my girls. Being a parent suits me, but the mid-drifts, the eyerolls, the sass … it's a bit much. I barely stop myself from rolling my own eyes when Lily comes out of the kitchen with a Tupperware full of cookies. Unlike her twin sister, my Lily prefers baggy hoodies to mid-drift shirts. I am so not ready for them to be teenagers.

"These are for Sarah. Aunt Charlie says chocolate chunk are her favourite." Lily stuffs the Tupperware into her backpack and pulls the strap over her shoulder.

I nod. "We are going to ride that way, but remember, I don't know if she's home."

After bumping into Sarah twice yesterday, I admit that I wouldn't mind seeing her again. She's funny in an awkward way, and I get the feeling she could use some friends in town. I'm always up for new friends. Plus, the girls are eager to help put Lena's gardens back together. They spent a lot of time there with Lena, learning about growing vegetables. Sarah's aunt was always a great influence on the girls.

"Do I have to wear a helmet?" Mari asks as she skips down the stairs in a longer mid-drift.

"Yes," I answer. "I'll let you slide on the knee pads, but helmets are non-negotiable."

"Fine." Mari pulls her earrings out of her pierced ears and tucks them into her pocket.

Lily already has her helmet on and is walking out the door. I glance at Jennifer's photo again. "This was your idea," I mumble under my breath.

I wasn't sold on being a dad until I became one. Even before the girls were born, hearing their heartbeats for the first time changed me. From that moment on, I was somebody's father, well, two somebodies. The only thing I didn't plan on was raising them alone. Some days it feels like they're raising me.

Although, there are still some things I'm teaching them, like how to care for their bikes. We each pause in the garage to check the tire pressure on the wheels. We ride together often enough that I am not worried about them being flat. I just want the girls to have good habits: check the tires, keep them clean, safety first. One day, when they have their driver's licenses, and I'm a tired old man, they'll be prepared for life. The girls may be a little less thorough than I'd like, though, as Lily and Mari take off before I finish checking over my bike.

Jumping on, I attempt to catch up with them. They're young enough that bike racing is a thrill. I keep them in sight but don't push too hard to catch up until they turn the corner. I follow along at a bit of a distance. The girls know the way to Lena's well.

As I come around the second turn, I panic for a moment when I see the girls' bikes tossed on the side of the road beside an older model Civic. I quickly realize they've found Sarah in her car, and Lily is already offering her cookies. But the scene doesn't quite make sense. They've never met Sarah and wouldn't talk to a stranger in their car, plus I don't know why she'd be parked on the side of the road right in front of her house. I pick up my pace, reaching the car a couple of minutes later.

"Is everything okay? Sarah, what's going on?" I ask, climbing off my bike.

I don't hear Sarah's response, but the girls go bananas. They both talk at once when they realize who she is. I let them go for a minute until I see Sarah wipe at a tear.

"Girls! Hey! I can't tell what you're saying when you talk at the same time."

"Sor-*ry*!" my dear princess Mari scoffs at me. She waves her hands in the air and walks back a couple of steps. "Lily swore she saw Lena. So we stopped and asked."

"Then we found out she was Sarah and we told her we had cookies," Lily adds.

"Okay." I take a breath, then focus back on Sarah. "What happened?"

She sniffs. "I hit a groundhog. I think he's dead."

Lily and Mari are both pointing. I walk around to see the damage. The very deceased groundhog is well off the road and there doesn't seem to be any damage to Sarah's car. When I walk back, Lily and Mari are on either side of Sarah, who's gotten out of the car. All three take a cookie from the container.

"You know, Charlie would be accusing the groundhog of denting her bumper," I say. This off the cuff remark is not received well by my estrogen filled audience. I hold up my hands in surrender. "Alright, I'm sorry. I'll bury him out here by the side of the road. Let me just go home and grab my truck and a shovel. Girls, you want to come with me?"

The twins shake their heads no.

"Sarah, can we see the gardens?" Lily asks.

Sarah sniffs again, trying to dry her eyes. It's kind of sweet how she cares about animals. First the mouse, now the groundhog. I wonder how a biology teacher who is this broken up over a rodent feels about dissecting frogs.

"Yes, sure, of course," Sarah responds.

"You girls go ahead. I'll catch up when I'm done here."

My girls are on their bikes before I say the word 'here'. Sarah watches them go.

"Oh, I still have her cookies," she says, turning back to me with the container in her hands.

I shrug. "They're for you anyway."

"I have a shovel, if that's easier," Sarah says as she opens her car door and slides in.

"Yeah," I nod. "I'll follow you and we'll take it from there."

I hop back on my bike and follow her car down her long driveway, past the orchard, and up to the small cottage-style house.

Grabbing the shovel Sarah offers me from the small shed around the side of the house, I walk back down her driveway to take care of the roadkill. When I finish and return to the cottage, I don't see anyone, so I replace the shovel in the shed and go back to knock on the front door. Lily opens it and invites me in. Mari is sprawled out on the couch, eating cookies. Sarah comes out of the kitchen wiping her hands dry on a towel. She motions to the door as Lily picks a cookie out of the Tupperware and plops onto the window seat overlooking the orchard.

Then to my girls, I say, "This doesn't look like the gardens you said you came to look at?"

They shake their heads without really looking up. Sarah walks to the front door and I turn to follow her out.

"Sorry about that," I point a thumb at the door as Sarah closes it. "They spent a lot of time over here. I was sorry to hear about Lena's passing. She was such a sweet and caring lady. The girls really took to her, and she was so good to them.

"I don't mind them hanging around. I didn't realize your twins were *the* twins." Sarah smiles. "Zia Lena told me a lot about them."

"Oh, I hope she only told you the good stories. Twins are often double the trouble, and they seem to find that trouble easily. One time Lena turned her back on the hose in the garden beds, and they had soaked each other before she even spun around," I reply.

"By the way, sorry about being such a mess out there. I'm not sure why I reacted that way. I know groundhogs get hit every day. I've just never hit one. It was a little more traumatizing than I expected," Sarah continues.

I nod, fighting a laugh. "Is it too early to make a joke about your pest control strategy? You've gone from catch and release to full frontal attack."

Sarah shakes her head at my lame attempt at humour, then replies, "Speaking of, I think the mouse is in the box thingy. Do you mind doing the honors?" Sarah asks, looking sheepish as she points to the kitchen cupboards.

"I don't mind at all."

I head into the kitchen and Sarah grabs an empty moving box from the back hallway. She gestures for me to put the trap in. I set the contraption in the box and place it by the door, planning to take it to a field on my way home. Sarah and I stand awkwardly looking at each other for a second before the twins come over

"Can we come help Sarah tomorrow after school?" Lily asks.

I shake my head. "No, stock order comes on Monday mornings, and you girls promised to work on the nuts and bolts for me. How else are you going to earn that allowance?"

Mari walks up behind Lily and scoffs. "It's an allowance. We're not supposed to earn it."

"Fine, I'll put you on payroll, take out taxes, and you can get half of what I'd normally give you. How does that sound?" I say with more attitude than I meant to show.

Sarah ducks her head. I can see her trying not to laugh as she scoots out of the kitchen and straightens a throw on the couch.

"What about Tuesday?" Lily tries again.

Mari jumps on the bandwagon. "Yeah, Dad, Tuesday?"

"You have to ask Sarah," I say, watching her come back into the kitchen. Her skirt sways as she walks, and I stare a bit too long. Both of my precious angels start laughing. Hopefully, not at my gawking.

"What?" Sarah asks.

"The girls have a question," I say, trying to avert everyone's attention.

Mari comes to my aid. "Can we come over on Tuesday?"

"Sure," Sarah smiles. "I'd like that."

I nod towards the door. "Come on, girls. We should get back."

No one actually wants to leave, but I can't come up with a good reason to continue invading Sarah's space. The girls trudge out the door.

"Thank you," Sarah says to me just before I follow them outside.

"Any time," I answer, thinking, hoping, there's another mouse somewhere else. Then I rescind that thought. She'll be by the store either way. The raised beds need rebuilding, and there's nowhere else in town to get lumber for that.

"I'll see you around," I say. Then, scooping up the mouse box, I pull the door closed behind me. I make it three whole steps before my darling daughters are giggling.

"What?" I scoff, trying to look imposing, but my girls know me too well. They keep laughing as they pedal away.

Chapter 4 - Sarah

As I pull into the hardware store parking lot, I am keenly aware that this is my third day in town and I've conveniently come up with a reason to see Austin a third day in a row. I know I'm lonely, but the hinge on the cabinet did fall off in my hand. When Charlie called me last night, I told her about the mouse and the groundhog but left out any mention of Austin. I feel like she's going to be plotting to set me up with someone, and she needs zero encouragement.

With the Ziploc bag containing the hinge and the screw that fell out with it, I walk inside. I don't see Austin, but I remember that the twins are supposed to be sorting nuts and bolts. I walk that way in denial of the fact that I hope to run into their dad again. I spot them in the last aisle, huddled up with rows of boxes on the tiny shelf in front of the wall of bins. I open my mouth to say hello, but I quickly realize something is wrong. Lily has her arms wrapped tightly around her waist.

Mari picks up a single screw and plops it into an open bin. "You can't keep running to the washroom every five minutes. You're going to look crazy, and you'll still ruin my jeans that you borrowed."

"I can't just tell Dad. This is so embarrassing." Lily leans her head on the bins in front of her.

I walk closer. "Girls, is everything okay?"

Mari turns and smiles brightly. "Sarah's here! She'll know what to do. Tell her."

Lily doesn't move. I have a strong suspicion of what this is all about, but I wait for her. Mari returns to dropping screws into bins. Lily sniffs and turns her head to look at me.

"I started my period," she mumbles.

"First time?" I ask, and she nods in response.

"Oh," I say, offering her a reassuring smile. "Let me see what I have in my purse."

Digging through my bag, I realize another trip to the grocery store might be in order. "Let me look in my car," I say.

Lily nods and curls against the wall again. I walk towards the front of the store, keys in hand. If I don't find anything in my car, which I don't think I will, I'll run to the grocery store. Ten feet from the door, Austin spots me.

"Hey, Sarah!" He waves a grill spatula at me.

Now, I'm a little embarrassed. What was I thinking coming here? I know what I was thinking. Quiet cottage, all alone, too many memories. I need to get my head together. I don't want him to think I am stalking him. Charlie made it awkward enough at our first meeting, and then I was a bit of a mess when I saw him yesterday.

Austin puts down the spatula and walks over. "How's it going? You didn't attack any more innocent wildlife, did you?"

I laugh and find a sliver of that thing I was really looking for, joy. I enjoy laughing, and Austin has a way of getting to the punch line. I'm not usually great at opening up to people, but Austin seems to have the ability to pull me out of my shell.

"No," I pause, considering how to tell him where I'm going. "I was about to run to the store for Lily."

"For Lily?" His eyebrows furrow. "What's up?"

I lean in to whisper, "She's gotten her first period."

Austin nods and walks behind the register. He produces a black Milwaukee tool bag about the size of a blow dryer case.

"Go ahead. Open it," he says, handing me the bag.

I unzip it to find a complete lineup of feminine care products, complete with Advil and chocolate. This is one serious dad. I find myself looking into his blue eyes and smiling at his thoughtfulness.

"I, um, will just go…" I point to the back of the store.

"Thanks, Sarah," he says, nodding. "I've had their Aunt Charlie talk to them about this kind of stuff because when I tried, they shut me down. Lily will be less embarrassed if you bring this back to them."

I shuffle to the back of the store, impressed and embarrassed all over again. At least Lily and I are in good company. She hasn't budged from her spot, even though Mari has worked her way down the line to the bolts.

"Hey," I say to Lily. "Everything you need, right here." I pass her the bag.

Lily runs her fingers over the embroidered word Milwaukee. I'm sure she knows where this came from, but she looks up at me. "Thanks, Sarah."

"You're welcome."

She tucks the bag under her arm and walks in the direction of the ladies' room. Mari continues working as if it's just another day. Curious and concerned, I walk over.

"How are you doing?" I ask, watching her sort the bolts like a pro.

Mari shrugs. "I'm okay."

"Is this the first for both of you?" I ask in a low voice.

Her lips kind of twitch as she thinks. "Yeah. I guess I should keep some stuff handy."

Mari's casual attitude seems genuine, but I can't help wondering if it is rehearsed. I remember being a wreck when I doubled over in gym class with cramps for the first time. Of course, it hasn't hit Mari yet.

"Well, if you or Lily ever need anything, don't hesitate to ask," I say.

I hope she knows I mean it. Their dad is obviously prepared, but some things are easier to say to a woman. Mari pauses in her work, propping an elbow on the box of bolts closest to her.

"You got that bag from Dad, didn't you?" Mari asks.

I nod. "Yeah."

"That's cool," she says. She returns to her work. "Thanks,"

she adds when I turn to walk away.

"You're welcome," I smile, but like a typical preteen, she doesn't look at me.

As I walk out of the aisle, I wonder how the girls are dealing with not having a mother at this stage of life. I can't imagine surviving middle school without Mamma and Zia Lena. I find Austin finishing up the grilling display, adding an Ole Smoky next to the Big Green Egg. I am surprised and impressed with how he handled such an important situation. Not a lot of guys have a power tool-branded bag full of stuff for periods.

"Hey," I say, walking up to him.

Austin nods to the back of the store. "How is she?"

"Good. Grateful, I'm sure." I stand there, twisting one flat on the polished floor, and I feel like I'm back in middle school gym class. "That's some pretty awesome parenting," I say, looking down into the half-empty tote he's working out of.

"Thanks. It's not easy, you know?" He reaches in and pulls out a few packs of matches, lining them up on the open grill top.

I bob my head, looking for the right words. I do not need to spill my guts right now about my loss. "Kind of, I guess. Teaching gives me some insight, but it's not the same. I kind of expected you to be more freaked out than the girls, honestly."

Austin chuckles. "I was, when they were four and started asking me where babies come from. I realized then I needed to know all about sensitive topics and how to talk to my girls. I got books, followed some blogs, learned how to braid hair and paint nails."

"Paint nails?" I ask, laughing.

"Hey," he points grill tongs at me. "I do a mean manicure!"

I crack up and have to catch my breath. "I might need to see this in action," I add when I can do so between chuckles. "Really, that's wonderful."

"Thanks," he laughs. "Parenting is the hardest job, especially when you know that your ultimate goal is to be put out of a job when they grow up and don't need you as much."

"Girls always need their dad. I speak from experience. It

may not be as hands-on, but I still have my dad on speed dial."

"Is speed dial still a thing?" Austin asks, raising his eyebrows.

"Ahhh," I huff another laugh. "Way to call me out!"

Then he laughs, and his smile makes those blue eyes stand out. A moment passes where I'm just admiring him. I clear my throat and look down at my shoes. Austin picks up a few grill brushes out of the tote, emptying it completely. He tucks them in various places around the display.

"I guess we'll go for some celebratory ice cream," he says, breaking up the awkward pause. "Hopefully, Ida's uncanny talent for reading what people need doesn't pick up on the change and suggest a different ice cream. That would embarrass the hell out of Lily!"

"Gosh, no," I say, shaking my head. "I was embarrassed when she called me out with a cup of chocolate peanut butter swirl. Does she do that with everyone?"

Austin chuckles. "It's uncanny how good she is at reading people. Maybe I'll call ahead to remind her that Lily's favourite is Strawberry and Mari's favourite is Bubble Gum, and we're sticking with those for now."

"Good idea." I nod, thinking I should try that, but she already knows what I like.

"Did you even find what you were looking for?" Austin asks, picking up the empty tote.

"Oh! No, I almost forgot." I pull the Ziploc out of my purse.

Austin turns it over in his hands. "I see. No wildlife, so you took it out on the kitchen cabinet?"

"I would never hurt Zia Lena's house!" I scoff, genuinely offended.

Then I laugh at the look on his face. He's holding back a chuckle. I just shake my head as he turns to walk to the back of the store, gesturing for me to come along. I follow him back down the center aisle towards the hardware section. We stop a few rows short of where Mari is working on nuts and bolts.

"The hinge is still intact, but I'm guessing the wood is

stripped." Austin picks up a small package with something that looks like a tiny cheese grater. "There're lots of ways to fix it, but if you cut a small piece of this and tuck it in the hole, you can reuse the old screw and it will match everything else."

"Oh, that's perfect," I say, taking the package from him. "I'd hate to have to change all of them to match, or change them at all."

"Charlie says you spent a lot of time with Lena," Austin says, changing the subject.

He folds his arms across his chest, and I am distracted by the muscles stretching out his flannel. I clear my throat and study the item in my hand.

"Yes, Zia Lena woke me up early every morning I stayed with her in the summers. We would weed or plant, depending on the need, for hours." I smile at the memory. "When we'd break for lunch, we'd start cookies before we ate, so they were still warm, fresh out of the oven. Her cookies were the best."

Austin nods. "She used to bake with the girls, too. They miss her an awful lot."

"I'm glad she got to spend time with them. I wish I had been around more the last few years." I suddenly feel adrift in my grief. Losing loved ones is never easy, no matter how old or how very young they are. Tears prick at my eyes, and I fight for a happy thought. "We used to go on bike rides in the afternoon or go to the beach. Osage is not a bad place to spend summers, especially after I started hanging out with Charlie and your brothers."

"Don't tell me you enjoyed putting up with those guys," he says with a smile.

I chuckle. "I was never bored trying to keep them out of trouble."

"If you like trouble, they'll be at Trivia night on Thursday." Austin touches his nose with his thumb, looking oddly tough for a man who does manicures on the side. "If you think you're up to the challenge."

"It's probably not as much of a fight as I'd have with

Charlie if I don't go. So…"

"Good," Austin smiles. "I look forward to seeing you there."

Chapter 5 - Austin

Two days have passed since I last saw Sarah. The girls have been at her cottage every day since Monday. When they came home last night talking about Sarah's plans for a greenhouse, I called to offer a professional assessment of the space. It's good business to be proactive in these situations. That's what I keep telling myself as I drive over to her house to lend my expertise.

I don't date, so what other motive could I have?

It took a few years after I lost Jennifer to even consider dating. In the small town of Osage, pickin's were slim, so I branched out. Huge mistake. City women weren't for me, and they certainly weren't going to tell me how to raise my girls. Technically, Sarah was from the city, but she seemed at home in Osage and not at all like a city girl.

What am I saying? I park my truck behind her Civic.

Knocking on the cottage door, I think about Lena. I can't say I knew her as well as the girls, but she left her mark on all of us. My eyes wander over the orchard where the trees are just starting to bud. It fared the best of all the garden space when she got sick, with the raised garden beds needing the most maintenance.

As I study the yard, the sun feels good on my face. I'm looking forward to summer and the busy season for the landscaping side of my business. I need to look at the applicants and hire a couple of assistants.

Where is she? I realize I've been standing on Sarah's porch for a while.

Perhaps I should check the raised gardens to see if she's already working on them this morning. I walk the length of the beds and find no one. Her car is here. She knows I'm coming. I figure she must be getting changed or something. I start walking back to the cottage when I notice a few hand tools out by one of the raised beds. The side has come off and dirt has fallen out, making a pile next to it.

"What do we have here?" I say, picking up a piece of the corner brace. Stainless steel. Good choice. Rust resistant and nontoxic.

I squat next to the warped piece of wood. The end is in good shape. The nails were really too short to begin with. The galvanized nails sitting by the hand tools were a much better length. Setting the brace in place, I drive a nail through the warped wood into the end of the side panel, then tug on the end to ensure that the fit is snug and tight. I drive a nail on the opposite side, and it's hard to tell the first piece was warped at all.

"Can I help you?" Sarah asks.

As I stand and turn, her face blushes. "Hey," I say, smiling. "Didn't mean to…"

"No," she laughs. "I just didn't recognize you from your behind- I mean. I didn't know it was you." Sarah holds her hands out, gesturing to the raised bed. "Go right ahead."

I chuckle and wave the hammer I'm still holding. "Well, since I started… You want to hold the next brace for me?"

"Sure." She steps over, and I see a pair of Crocs peek out from under the long skirt she's wearing. She kneels in the dirt and sets the brace against the raised bed.

I admire her willingness to get dirty and work. *Not too city then,* and this time I don't bother to correct the thought. I squat next to her and drive the next nail. We work side by side for a while, shoring up this bed and shoveling the dirt back into place. Sarah stands back, dusting dirt off her hands.

"Thanks."

"You're welcome," I smile and pick up the other hand

tools. "These go in the lean-to?"

"Yes."

We walk side by side, and I notice how easy we are together. I'm glad Sarah decided to move into Lena's. I'm also glad she's willing to have the girls around.

"Thank you," I say. "For letting Mari and Lily hang around."

"Oh, no. Thank you. They've been a great help and fun company. Where are they today?" Sarah asks.

"With Charlie. She's got the afternoon off." We end our walk past the last garden bed in an open area that looks like the perfect spot for a greenhouse.

Sarah looks over the area with her hands on her hips. "That's right, shopping."

"Shopping," I repeat. "Hopefully for something that's not a mid-drift."

"I'm not sure I would trust Charlie with that mission," Sarah says with a laugh.

"Yeah," I huff. "So, this is where you want to build a greenhouse?"

"Yes, I think there's room for a sixteen foot diameter geodome here. What do you think?"

Before I answer, Sarah steps over to a patch of straw.

"But I'm trying to save this butterfly bush. I pruned it back, but I think it'll survive." She walks across the space and points to another patch of something that could be a plant. "And the Black-eyed Susan here. I could transplant it, but it's well established."

I nod, enjoying her enthusiasm. "Sure. That will make it a tight fit, but you could still do it. You'll want to be careful grading the area. What kind of foundation are you thinking of?"

"Wood, definitely."

"Okay, so, grading, wood foundation. I'd recommend landscape fabric go down to prevent weeds from coming up. You'll also need a barrier between your foundation and your greenhouse."

"Because of the arsenic in pressure-treated wood?" Sarah asks.

"No, they stopped using arsenic in 2005. Now wood is treated with copper, which is less poisonous, but is corrosive to aluminum. If you're interested, there're other weather-resistant woods that don't have any chemicals. Cedar is a great choice," I offer.

"Is it expensive?" Sarah asks. Then she holds up her hands. "I want to do this right, but you know, on a teacher's salary."

"Sure. I understand. You could use pressure-treated wood for the bottom and cedar for the barrier. If you want to save money on grading, I could rent you a skid steer."

Sara's eyes go wide. "I don't know about that."

"You could do it. I'd be happy to show you how to use it. It's the least I could do for letting the girls invade your life every day."

"You don't owe me a thing. I promise. Zia Lena thought the world of them, and I can see why."

I smile, feeling that proud papa feeling in my chest. "They are great kids."

As the conversation lulls, I notice a small black cat nearby. A closer look reveals it to be a squirrel, foraging in the weeds near what used to be a flower bed.

"Careful," I say as he ventures closer. I point a thumb at Sarah as she leans to see what I'm looking at. "This one has it out for your kind."

I get a slap on the arm from Sarah. I'm pleasantly surprised by her strength and the peel of laughter she lets out. I turn to her, chuckling. "Hey, give the squirrel a chance!"

She starts walking towards the cottage and I fall into step next to her.

"I'm still not convinced about the skid steer," she says, a faint smile still on her lips.

I rub a hand over my beard and let out another chuckle. "Yeah, I'm sure the squirrel will feel safer without you behind the wheel, too."

She slaps my arm again as we turn to walk inside the cottage. Sarah starts the kettle for tea, and I make myself at home at the small table. A jar in the center reveals homemade chocolate chip cookies, and she gestures for me to help myself.

"These are good," I mumble over a bite.

Sarah pulls out two mugs. As she sets out cream and honey on the table next to me, she pulls a cookie out of the jar.

"I still feel bad," she says before taking a delicate bite.

"For what?" I ask.

Her index finger touches her lips, and my eyes linger there, admiring the curve of her plump bottom lip.

"The groundhog," she says.

My eyes drift up to her deep brown eyes. "Oh," I shrug. "Nothing you could do about it. Better you hit one than swerve to miss it and get hurt."

Sarah sighs. "I guess."

The kettle sings, and she pops the last bite of cookie in her mouth before pouring hot water into the mugs. With one in each hand, she joins me at the table. I feel so comfortable here with her, like we've been at this for years.

What am I saying?

I laugh at myself for being so whimsical.

"Do you really think I could do the grading myself?" Sarah asks, pulling a second cookie out of the jar.

I smile. "Absolutely." *And if not, I'd enjoy watching you try.* "I'm glad to help, too. It's not as complicated as you'd think."

"Alright, I guess-"

"How about Sunday?" I offer before she has a chance to finish answering.

Sarah smiles. "Okay, but I'm trusting you to help me keep the Black-eyed Susans safe." She points a finger at me.

I point a finger right back. "And the squirrels. Don't forget them."

Our laughter comes easily. For the next hour we run through a few tea bags each and the rest of the cookies. The conversation rolls easily through topic after topic until a phone call from the store interrupts us, but I need to head back anyway.

Sarah stands to walk me out. I reluctantly do the same. Taking a look around the cottage, I think how pleasant it is and feel hesitant to leave.

Is it the cottage or the company? But the answer is obvious. I shove my hands in my pockets, like a fifteen-year-old asking a girl out on a date for the first time. *This is not a date. We are not dating. I don't date,* I remind myself.

"So, trivia tonight?"

Sarah's face scrunches up like she just tasted something awful. "I guess," she says, letting her nose and eyes relax.

I try to act casual. "I just know Charlie wants you there. Noah and William would love to see you, too."

"Yeah, okay. Seven, right?"

"Every Thursday, rain or shine." I reach for the door. "You can't tell me you don't like trivia."

"I love trivia. It's not that. I don't know." Her thoughts and her words trail off.

I sense there's more to Sarah's story than inheriting a house and moving to the country. *There's always more to the story.*

"I'll see you," I glance down at my watch. "In a couple hours. Where does the time go?"

As I walk out, I think about where the time actually went. We'd sat at that table for more than an hour. More like two hours and some change. It didn't feel like it. I find myself looking forward to trivia more than usual as I pull up to the store just in time to lock up for the day.

Chapter 6 – Sarah

"I do love trivia," I mumble, trying to convince myself as I park outside the sandbar.

I don't know what my deal is. I used to love stuff like this, and these are friends. Granted, I haven't seen them in a while, but I should be looking forward to this. Why am I so uncertain these days?

A long look at the front entrance of the Sandbar reminds me of Saturday, the day I arrived. The feelings surface like driftwood on the lake.

I am a divorcee; I made this choice. I have to move on. Fresh start.

My feet finally start moving towards the door, and I let out a sigh of relief.

Inside, the Sandbar smells of beer and deep-fried foods. My stomach growls as I scan for anyone I may know. All the feelings and sadness drop away at the sound of a familiar voice.

"Well, fuck a duck, if it isn't Sarah the Terror!"

"Hey, Noah," I hold out my arms for a hug as I walk closer.

Austin's younger brother stands from the round table he is sitting at and wraps his arms around me, lifting me off the floor and swinging me in a low circle. For a moment, I feel like a kid again, happy and free. My feet land with a plop next to Noah's twin.

"How'd you know it wasn't me?" William asks, laughing. He stands up to put an arm around my shoulders.

I squeeze him tight before poking him in the ribs. "For starters, your hair has been shorter since eighth grade. Second,

Noah is the only one who calls me *Sarah the Terror*." A misnomer if you ask me, I was an angel as a teenager. Kept this crew out of so much trouble. "We're not repeating your nickname for me in mixed company."

He leans down to whisper it in my ear. I laugh loudly enough to drown out the words.

"Hey!" a voice scolds.

I look up to see Austin sitting beside Noah with an oddly serious expression. Then, his smile comes out. "No secrets. Out with it, Will."

William flashes me with a coy smile. He winks as he sits back down, ignoring Austin's demand.

"No cavorting with the enemy!" Charlie yells from halfway across the bar.

She arrives at the boys' table with a round of beer and a plate of loaded cheesy fries. I grab a spud, stuffing it in my mouth as she sets the tray down. Charlie begins passing out beers, and I take a second fry. Austin reaches across the table and snatches the plate away.

"Those are mine," he says, narrowing his eyes at me. "Thank you very much."

I reach past Noah and grab a couple more. "No, thank you." I give him a sweet smile and munch away on the fries.

Austin's eyes meet mine and I'm pleasantly lost for a moment. His blue irises are striking against his dark hair and beard. They're a light icy colour throughout but rimmed by a darker cobalt blue, giving his eyes a halo look. I'm mesmerized.

"Over here," Charlie says, breaking into my thoughts.

She sets a beer down at the table next to the guys and motions to an empty chair. I pull it closer to Austin and sneak another fry off his plate.

"I'll be back. Try not to tear the place down while I'm gone." Charlie eyes Noah, knowing that he is usually the troublemaker.

I notice William watching her leave. When he looks back to the table and finds me watching, he nods ever so slightly.

Things haven't changed much between us over the years. William may have given me the nickname, *Sexy Ass Sarah*, but we both knew it was a cover up for his true feelings. Feelings that were 100% not about me.

I understood why he didn't ask Charlie out when we were younger. William knew she couldn't see anyone beyond his little brother. Once Charlie married Zach, William seemed to get over her, but I guess that was a cover up too. Zach's passing years ago devastated the Moore family, not to mention Charlie, his sweetheart.

"Save me a few, will ya?" Austin says.

I look down and see his half-empty plate and a few fries in my hand as I munch. "I shared my cookies," I say innocently enough.

Noah picks up right where we left off. "Cookies? Is that what they're calling it these days?"

"Shut up!" I say, laughing and blushing furiously. Leave it to Noah to make something as simple as cookies into a sexual innuendo.

A petite, dark-haired woman sits down at my table. I notice Noah glance up and roll his eyes at her arrival. William acknowledges her with a smile and another polite nod, a warm welcome from him. I wonder about the strange dynamic between her and Noah, though. Always the class clown, the life of the party, it's unlike him to brush someone off. The woman looks away, apparently searching the bar for someone else to talk to.

I absentmindedly reach for another fry and my fingers hit the table. I look over to see Austin holding his plate off to the side, giving me the stink eye. When I let out a cackle, he slides the plate back over to me.

"Thanks," I mumble over another bite.

Charlie reappears with a mixed drink and sets it in front of the newcomer. "Lauren, this is your new teammate, Sarah. Sarah, this is Lauren. She's a math teacher at Osage Secondary School."

"Oh, great. I'll be teaching there this fall," I say, reaching out my hand.

Lauren and I shake, but before she can answer, a dark shadow looms over the table. Connor, the oldest of the Moore brothers, slides into the chair on the other side of Austin, his piercing blue eyes taking me in.

"Hey, Sarah, right?" he says with as much warmth as river rock. I'm surprised he knows my name. Although Austin or the twins might have mentioned seeing me. If I weren't sitting with his brothers, I never would have recognized him.

"Hey," I say, turning my attention back to Lauren, but another familiar face arrives.

I can't remember Mr. Moore's first name, but his smile reminds me of Austin and Noah. Ida follows him in, and the table erupts in greeting. She hugs all the Moore boys before joining Lauren and me.

"Charlie, can I get two more orders of fries?" Austin asks.

"Damn, hungry today?" she asks.

Austin turns his head slowly to stare at me. "Starving."

"Guess you won't be needing these." I slide his nearly empty plate my way and set it on the table with Lauren. "Fries?" I ask.

She chuckles and takes one. A scuffing sound accompanies Austin as he slides his chair closer to mine and grabs a couple of fries off his stolen plate.

"Hey, I was thinking on Sunday I'd bring the skid steer. What do you think?" Austin's easy smile as he pilfers his own fries warms my heart.

"Sounds great." I know I'm grinning, like wide-eyed, starstruck grinning. I don't know what it is about Austin that makes me feel like laughing is the only logical answer.

Charlie clears her throat loudly. "Thinking of jumping ship, Moore?"

Austin shrugs. "Just following my food."

She holds a box out in front of us. Austin pulls his cell phone out and drops it in. Lauren and Ida follow suit.

"What's this?" I ask.

"House rules. Prevents cheating." Austin reaches back to his table for his beer. "And, you know, antisocial behavior."

Charlie shakes the box in front of my face. "Come on. Cough it up. Like you need the help. The only one who gets to keep his phone is Connor, because he's always *on call*," she says with just a hint of sarcasm.

I pull my phone out of my purse and drop it in. Charlie grins as she glances past me to where Austin is leaning on the table, sipping his beer. Oh great, Charlie is going to read into this. Now I feel heat on my face. Imagining the blush creeping up my neck and cheeks, I take a long sip of my beer.

The ice-cold tang tastes good. It feels good going down. It's been a long time since I drank. Not good for fertility. *Not an issue today*, I remind myself. I haven't made the appointment yet. Fertility specialists are expensive. So is in vitro fertilization, but it results in what I want, what I've always wanted.

"Biology. Right, Sarah?" Austin nudges me.

"What?" I look around and realize that Lauren and Ida are watching me, waiting for an answer to a question I didn't hear while lost in thought.

"You're going to be teaching biology at Osaga?" Lauren offers.

I start nodding before I find the word I'm looking for. "Yes," I say stupidly. Then I laugh at myself. "Sorry. Long day."

"Do any damage? Do I need to come check on the squirrel?" Austin asks.

I roll my eyes. "No, thank you." I give my attention to Lauren since something about Austin distracts me to the point of confusion. "How long have you taught at Osage?"

"Ten years. As long as I've been teaching, really."

"Austin, you're on our team, remember," Noah says with less humor than usual.

Lauren huffs. "Better get back to team Needs to Know Moore." She smiles at Austin somewhat genuinely.

Austin gives me a look like he's a cat trapped between a

bucket of water and a rocking chair. "Good luck," he tells me before sliding his chair back to his table.

"Alright, everybody!" Charlie yells from a few feet away. "Tonight, we have at Table One, Know Moores! Table Two, Momma's Turn to Get Rowdy."

A table of women on the far side of the room cheers. Charlie throws a fist up in solidarity, then returns to her index cards.

"Table Three, MIT Bound and Determined." A round of cheers comes from a younger-looking group.

"Table Four, Another Round of Pi!" Charlie plops the index cards down.

Noah scoffs at the team name for my table, and I realize that Pi is the mathematical term, not the dessert. Lauren sits up straighter with a smirk.

"Last call for the kitchen before we get started," Charlie tells the room.

Momma's Turn to Get Rowdy waves, and she heads over to take their order. A tall, lanky man appears with two plates of loaded fries. He sets them both in front of Austin. With a dramatic show, Austin moves one plate away then sets the other in front of me.

"That's it. We are officially enemies until the end of trivia. No cheating off me or my fries." He winks and shifts back into his chair.

Laughing, I lift my beer in a toast. Then I slide the fries towards Lauren and Ida, offering to share. Ida gives me a knowing look and I just shrug. It's good to be back with the Moore men and Charlie. I didn't realize how much I missed all of them. Austin and I had never been close as teenagers. As the older two, Connor and Austin didn't hang out with Charlie and I as much as the twins and Zach, but he is quickly growing on me.

"As always, you have sixty seconds to answer on the paper in front of you. No cheating, Noah. First question: What's another name for a garbanzo bean?"

Chapter 7 - Austin

"You gonna help us out, bro?"

I turn my head towards William just as Noah passes Charlie our answer on the little slip of paper. "Sorry. Missed that one."

"Right," Connor scoffs. "What planet are you on tonight?"

I shrug and nurse my beer, trying not to stare too long in the other direction at a certain brunette with all the answers. I'm not usually much help with trivia anyway, unless it's a hardware-related question.

"The answer is *galvanized!*" Charlie yells over the jukebox.

Yup, I should have been paying attention to that one. I give Connor another shrug. He just shakes his head and folds his arms.

"That puts Another Round of Pi in the lead!" Charlie cheers with the ladies at the table next to ours. "Next question and the last one in this round: Where would one find the smallest bone in the human body?"

I know Sarah knows the answer to this question. When I look over at her, I see Noah doing the same thing he's been doing for half the night. He's leaning back in his chair, whispering in her ear. Sarah's laugh is sweet, but I find myself annoyed with my brother. Then I realize what's happening. Noah is telling her jokes as he peeks at her answers.

"Damn," I huff under my breath. *What am I thinking? Am I really jealous of Noah?*

Charlie begins collecting the papers with team answers signaling the end of the round, and I stand abruptly, too abruptly. The whole table turns to see what I'm doing. "I need another beer," I say. "Anyone else?"

William nods, and I nod back. Then, I step between Sarah and Noah, causing the front legs of his chair to hit the hardwood floor with a heavy smack. "What about you?" I ask, putting a hand on her shoulder.

"Sure," she looks up with a smile that causes her eyes to sparkle.

I find myself grinning like a fool as I make my way up to the bar. Duke raises his glass to me as I lean on the high-top, waiting for Scott to come out of the kitchen. When he does, I simply hold up three fingers and he starts pouring.

After delivering William and Sarah their beers, I sit down, determined to ignore Noah. He's flirting, yes, but he flirts with everyone. Except Lauren. He has *never* flirted with Lauren. No one knows what she did to unearth the bad side none of us knew Noah had, but those two need a referee anytime they are forced to interact.

As long as it's not me.

"Did you look at Eric's application?" Connor asks.

I shake my head. "Not yet. I need to work on that."

He taps the table between us. "Start with his. I owe his dad a favour."

"So, the guy pulled your balls out of a house fire, and I'm stuck with his son forever?" I raise my eyebrows, trying not to smirk at Connor. He wouldn't appreciate it.

My big brother leans back and folds his arms. "Yeah, so call him. This week."

"Is he even going to be able to do the job? I don't need another cashier. I need someone who can haul fertilizer and not cry about it."

"He can handle the work," Connor says flatly.

I know from experience that our discussion is over. I also know that Connor wouldn't say the kid could handle it if he couldn't. I don't mind, really. Hiring a high schooler for the summer and training him right means I'll probably have great help for the next few busy seasons.

"Boys, are you fighting?" Charlie asks, giving Connor a squinting stare.

My brother smiles, just for her. I imagine if we'd ever had a little sister growing up, Connor would have been a soft touch, like he is with Charlie. She's been family for so long, it's kind of like we grew up with a sister. He also lets my girls get away with murder. Makes my job harder sometimes, but it's nice to see this side of him instead of his usual grumpy self.

"Not fighting today, Charlie. How about some of those fries like you gave Austin earlier?"

"Comin' right up. Austin?" she asks, turning towards me.

"I'm good. Thanks, Charlie."

She moves on to the next table, taking orders before the next round of trivia starts. The room gets louder as people use the break to talk about other stuff. Team *Momma's Turn to Get Rowdy* attempts to live up to its name as they all trip to the jukebox, beer in hand.

"Austin?" I turn to see Ida smiling wide. "Do you have a minute?"

"Sure." I stand and pull out the chair next to Sarah. "What's up?" I ask as I sit.

"I could use your advice about the shop. I know you don't do remodeling per se, but the lights seem to be all going out at the same time."

Ida doesn't quite ask a question, and I sense this is going to be a long conversation. I stretch behind me to grab my beer, and Connor helps out by pushing it closer. I get comfortable, stretching my arm across the back of Sarah's chair. "Which lights are we talking about?"

Ida smiles widely, and her eyes dart to Sarah, who's deep in conversation with Lauren about Osage Secondary School. I am starting to suspect a setup. I'm okay with it, I decide. I lean closer to Sarah purely to appease Ida. So, I tell myself.

When Sarah glances at me and smiles, Ida continues. "Well, the overhead lights, you know the yellowish looking ones?"

"The fluorescent lights, you mean?"

"Yes, those. I just think they take away from the natural light. What can I do about that?"

An open-ended question, if ever there were one. I think for a minute and start to nod. The lights in the store are outdated. Switching to LEDs would lower the electric bill.

"What's your budget look like for this project?" I ask. "Are you going to pay an electrician?"

"I can help," Dad offers before Ida can answer.

The woman's cheeks flush slightly. "Thank you, Cal."

"So, labor is covered," I nod, knowing that means me taking a day off to hold the ladder for Dad.

"Nachos!" Charlie chimes, setting a plate in front of Sarah.

"Thanks," she says. "We still on for tomorrow? I'll pick up Lily and Mari on my way over in the morning."

"Yes, I bought cookie dough, frozen pizza, and seed packets. We're all set."

"Great." Charlie motions to me with her chin. "Make sure they get up, okay?"

"Yeah, no problem," I answer, making a mental note to ask the girls about their Friday plans. I guess I won't have help tomorrow after all.

Charlie skips to the next table, balancing a tray of food like a circus performer spinning plates.

It's a wonder she doesn't sling stuff everywhere.

Then, Sarah slides the plate closer to me. "Nachos?" she asks.

Her brown eyes catch mine. A sensation I haven't experienced in a long time creeps across my chest. It feels good to be around her. Too good. Another more personal sensation strikes, and I shift in my chair, returning my attention to Ida.

"LED's," I say before stuffing a nacho in my mouth.

"LED's?" Ida asks.

I nod, shift again, and relax as the tension subsides. "They use less electricity. Could save you some money, and they come in natural light shades. We'll have to swap out the ballasts."

"I like the idea of saving on electricity," Ida says.

Charlie is calling out the scores and setting up for round two. I decide to stay put and ask Ida what else the shop might need while we're pricing light fixtures. I won't make any money because Dad will insist I sell to her at cost. The real benefit to me is enjoying Sarah's smile over Connor's scowl.

Chapter 8 - Sarah

Sipping my chamomile tea, I step out into the crisp spring air. The orchard is full of buds. A few of the pears need pruning, but the apple trees are in great shape. I pause at the edge of the tree line and think about going back to make breakfast. I have great plans for today and look forward to having Charlie, Mari, and Lily's help.

Instead, I walk steadily out amongst the fruit trees, reaching up to touch the soft new growth as I pass. I wonder if plums could survive the winter if I plant them within the protection of the Macintosh apples. Steam curls upward from my favourite mug, and the deep inhale I pull reveals the scent of spring and soil. I close my eyes, taking another full breath. I feel at home.

This is where I belong.

I open my eyes when I hear the sound of gravel popping under tires. Charlie's Land Rover comes bouncing into view. I feel my lips curve up into a smile. The quiet is definitely over for the day, but I'm glad she's here. As I walk slowly back to the cottage, I see the girls climb out of the SUV and let themselves into the house.

Charlie follows, but must realize I'm not there. She comes back out about the time I pass the cars on my way to the porch.

"Everything okay?" she asks.

"Yup." I nod and sip my tea. "Just savoring the morning, the way Zia Lena taught me to."

Charlie smiles and throws an arm around my shoulders. "Good. Are you also planning on cooking breakfast the way she taught you to? Because I could use an omelet."

We both laugh as we step inside. "I suppose we could make breakfast. Who wants to chop veggies?"

"Veggies for breakfast?" Mari asks, making a face.

Lily is already walking around the counter into the kitchen.

"Let's wash up," I say softly.

Before long, each of us has a task and a cup of tea. I feel a little like Ida as I correctly guess Chai for Mari and Lavender Green Tea for Lily. I also set aside a few bags of raspberry leaf tea for her to take with her, since it's so good for women's health. Lily only nods in response to the gesture, but I sense she is still grateful. Zia Lena's small table is soon overflowing with toast, jam, omelets, and teacups. She would have loved this little gathering.

"So, girls, how's school going?" I ask as I spread butter on my toast.

"Good," Mari answers with a shrug.

Lily looks away, tapping her plate absentmindedly with her fork. I glance at Charlie, then at Mari.

"Lily doesn't love school. She has dyslexia," Mari offers.

"Oh," I smile at Lily. "That's nothing to be ashamed of."

"Can we talk about something else?" she mumbles.

"Sure," I nod. I'd love to talk to her about it, but obviously that is a conversation for another time. "What do you like to do in your free time?"

The girls begin talking over one another about gymnastics. I nod along for a minute as they tell me all the exercises they do and what equipment is the most fun.

"We only do that during the school year, though," Mari says with a slight pout.

"Oh, what do you do during the summer?" I ask.

"Soccer," Lily says, smiling.

It's good to see her excited about something. "What position do you play?"

"Midfielder. Coach asked me to be goalie next year."

"Wow! That's great. Mari, do you play too?" I ask.

"Nope."

Charlie cocks her head. "She's too cool for that."

Mari offers another one of her shrugs, taking a bite of her omelet.

"What do you do for fun?" Lily asks.

It's such a simple question, but I stumble with the thought. What do I do for fun? What brings me joy? I don't know that I have felt joyful for quite a while; could I get there again? Zia Lena's gardens make me cheerful, and I'm enjoying being in Osage and spending time with Charlie. For the first time in a long time, I can imagine myself feeling joy.

While I am contemplating my lightheartedness, Charlie comes to my rescue. "Most recently, Sarah enjoyed kicking your dad's butt in trivia."

I laugh. "It was so great seeing all the guys together again. I can't imagine what it was like to have all five of them in one house."

"The five of them?" Lily asks.

Mari elbows here. "She's including Uncle Zach."

"Oh, what was he like?" she asks innocently.

I glance at Charlie just in time to see her eyes turn glassy.

"He was wonderful. Perhaps I can tell you a few stories about him later. You girls about ready to play in the dirt?"

Mari and Lily nod. Charlie holds it together, though I know she's hurting. I loved Frank, deeply. Our divorce nearly killed me, but even our years together were nothing like what Charlie and Zach had.

We finish our breakfast quickly and quietly. I send the girls out to fetch the tools from the lean-to before turning my attention to Charlie.

"I'm so sorry. I wasn't thinking."

"No," she shakes her head as a few tears slip out. "I want to talk to them about him. I want to tell them everything about their-"

I pull Charlie into a hug. She squeezes me tight, and I

remember all the late nights we spent just crying together after Zach died.

Eighteen is too young. Too young to die and too young to lose someone you love.

Charlie resumes her brave face and swipes at one last tear. "Let me clean up. I'll be out in a minute."

"Sure," I say, forcing a smile.

Stepping out into the bright spring sun, I feel out of place. The person I lost was so much younger. I lay a hand on my stomach and swallow a knot in my throat. The sight of the girls digging in the dirt of one of the garden beds redirects my focus. Now, I am looking forward to teaching the girls Zia Lena's tried and true method for planting carrots. I push the lingering blues away.

No more of that today.

"Okay, today we are going to work on carrots and lettuce," I say as I kneel next to Lily. "Mari, there is a coffee can with seeds in the lean-to. Will you grab it?"

Mari dashes off, giving Lily and me a short moment alone.

"You know, Lily, you can talk to me about school if you want. Dyslexia isn't the end of the world, especially if you know how to advocate for yourself."

She nods without taking her eyes off the dirt. Pulling her fingers through the soft, black soil, thin rows form. Then, Lily smooths it back out again. I can't count the number of times I've done the same thing. Even though I wish she would open up, I can appreciate the lure of the earth and planting as a distraction from just about anything.

Mari returns and passes me the old coffee can that Zia Lena kept her seeds in. I've bought fresh seeds, and the packets look oddly bright against the slightly yellow and rusted can. I smile as I think about the next step: the water hose.

How many times has this gone awry? Hopefully, the girls don't end up soaking me or each other.

"Okay, first, we need to get the soil nice and wet. Lily, will you turn the water hose on?"

I stand and set the seeds on the next garden bed over, where they will be relatively safe from errant water spray. By the time we finish with the hose, Charlie comes out of the cottage.

"Hey," she says softly as she steps up next to me.

I look into her eyes and see the redness, but they are dry now. "Hey," I answer, putting an arm around her.

"I see we managed this without showers today." Charlie attempts a smile to go with the quip.

Mari giggles. Lily bites her lip but still grins. I remember Austin telling me about them soaking each other the way their uncles did when we were younger. My heart flutters suddenly as I find myself thinking about his blue eyes.

"You okay, Sarah?" Mari asks. She's staring at me with her head tilted.

I clear my throat, shaking off the distraction. "Yes, I'm great. Um–" I look at Charlie, who laughs at my flustered expression.

She nudges me with her hip as she laughs. "Come on, Mari. Let's roll up the water hose."

As they work on that, Lily and I begin making shallow rows in the dirt for the carrot seeds. She follows my lead without being told what to do, and I wonder what she's thinking. As a teacher, I can tell she's intelligent, but there's only so much I can do from the outside looking in.

Maybe she just needs more time. I can relate to that.

"You're doing great, Lily. We don't want to bury the seeds. We just want enough of a row that we know where we're planting."

Mari and Charlie return, and I begin passing out seeds to all three of them.

"They're so small," Lily says, pushing the seeds back and forth with her index finger.

I nod, feeling the joy we were talking about earlier. *Planting brings me joy.*

"They are, but they'll bring nice big carrots if we do this right. Now, gently sprinkle the tiny carrot seeds along the rows we've made. Don't press them into the dirt. Let them sit on top." Between the four of us, we finish laying out seeds quickly. "Girls, follow me."

We walk back to the lean-to where Zia Lena kept her boards. The one-by-sixes are perfect for this because they are long but lightweight.

"Can you each carry one?" I ask, handing a board to Mari.

She purses her lips and nods, marching away. Lily takes the second board from me, and her nose wrinkles up.

"Too heavy?" I ask.

Lily shakes her head. "It feels like it will give me a splinter."

"Oh, no problem. Set it down." I duck into the lean-to and find Zia Lena's garden gloves. Whacking them on my skirt, I knock the dust and cobwebs off. "Here."

Pulling the gloves on, Lily smiles at the green with pink polka dots. "I love green."

"That was Zia Lena's favourite colour," I say, enjoying talking about her to someone who knew her.

Lily lifts the board. "I remember." Then she marches off like Mari.

I grab a third board and follow. At the garden bed, I lay the first board down. "Place them over the seeds but remember not to press them into the soil. Let them lay softly on top. These boards will keep the soil nice and moist for seed germination. And, since we've already watered well, we don't need to water again. We'll just check under the boards every day, making sure the area stays damp. When the tiny carrot seeds start to sprout, we'll remove the boards."

"That's cool," Mari says, placing her board next to mine. "You should make a YouTube video of this."

Charlie laughs before I have a chance to reveal my camera shyness. "Maybe you could make a video of it," she tells Mari.

"Nah," she shakes her head. "I'm not great at teaching things like Sarah."

"Thanks." I stand up straighter at the compliment. "I'm not sure I'm ready for internet stardom, though."

As Lily places her board onto the garden bed, I clap my hands together. "Who's ready to work on lettuce?"

Chapter 9 - Sarah

The Coach Diner has the same feel as every small town dinner I've ever been to. There's no facade, literally or figuratively. The walls are sheet rock, painted light beige, and the decor is mostly posters from local events long past. Still, it's nice being in a place with little pretense. Especially, as I notice dirt stains on my dress. I brush at them to no avail when a familiar face appears by the unattended hostess stand.

Austin smiles when he sees me and walks over. Standing, I reach to hug him like I would Noah or William, but when he returns the embrace, it feels different. I feel different.

"How are you?" he asks, stepping back.

I sit back down, trying to ignore my elevated pulse, and motion for him to join me. "Good and tired. How are you?"

"Ditto." Austin shrugs off his jacket and sits down across from me.

My waitress returns with my order, a grilled cheese with a side of sliced tomatoes. I wonder if I look silly ordering something so simple. I just didn't feel like cooking. I know it's an excuse. The reality is I was lonely, and Charlie was unavailable to hold my hand. So, I came here just to be around people. Besides, after a long day in the garden, I really didn't feel like cooking.

"Fish and chips," Austin says.

I realize I did it again, completely checked out of my surroundings. Fortunately, neither Austin nor the waitress seem to have noticed. She slips her book back into her apron and heads towards the kitchen. Austin turns his blue eyes and warm smile on me, and I feel like the cheddar oozing onto the plate in front of me.

"Grilled cheese?" he asks as one side of his mouth hikes up a little higher with his grin.

"Yup," I answer with my own smile. I feel the heat creeping up my neck, but I ignore it. "The sourdough here is so good."

"It is pretty good." Austin leans back in his chair, folding his arms comfortably across his broad chest. "How's the progress on the garden going?"

"Great," I mumble over a bite of my sandwich. I quickly dab at my lips, laughing at how stupidly delicious this sandwich is. "I have sown three varieties of lettuce, carrots, and just put in the seedling tomatoes I bought from the nursery. The orchard is doing well. I think I'll need to take out one of the pear trees. It's looking very rough."

"Do you think it's sick?" Austin asks.

"Sick?" I'm surprised at the question.

The waitress brings Austin's Coke and refreshes my water. My mouth waters a bit as I watch him enjoy a long sip from the sweet drink. Pops of all kinds have been on my list of foods to avoid for so long.

"Yeah, you know with a fungus or something that can spread to the other trees?"

"Oh, no. I don't think so, but several of the branches are clearly dead. I don't see much new growth."

"Maybe we can save it. Prune it back, add fertilizer." Austin leans his elbows on the table, bringing those blue eyes incredibly close.

I find myself lingering on the word *we*. I like the sound of it. I am relearning how to be independent, but sometimes it's nice to be part of a team, shared responsibility and all. With Austin, it feels like we're in this together. Now, I'm staring. I take a bite of my sandwich, pretending to process his suggestion. Really, I'm surprised he thought of it. I like that he knows so much about trees and gardens. But I know I'm just being silly, thinking about *we*. I shake my head slightly.

"Are you sure?" he asks. "Lena always took such good care of that orchard."

I start nodding instead of shaking my head, trying to focus on what he's asking rather than the fantasy playing out in my head. "Yes, she did. Maybe I'll try that first."

"Good. We can look at it tomorrow."

"Tomorrow?" I ask. Shuffling my feet, I feel Austin's foot brush against mine. *Oh, no. Now I'm playing footsie! Get it together, Sarah.* But even as I scold myself, his foot rubs against my ankle. Melting like the cheese all over again, I decide to just be still and pretend I don't notice how close we are to each other. "What's tomorrow?"

"Oh, no you don't, Sarah. You are not chickening out on me." He leans back as the waitress sets a plate of food in front of him. Austin reaches across to the empty table next to ours to grab a bottle of malt vinegar. "I've already got the skid steer loaded and the blueprints for your geodome. You can do this."

I nearly jump as I process his words. "Wait, you already have blueprints?"

"Yeah." He shrugs nonchalantly, shaking vinegar over his fish. "I ordered them and the windowpanes after we met on Thursday. I got them printed, and the supplies should be delivered later next week."

"But, how much is all that? I mean, I can pay you, but-" I stop when Austin shakes his head.

"Don't worry about it. We'll work it out. Besides, I plan on milking you for free tutoring for the next six or seven years," he says the last part with a wink.

I can always count on a Moore to make me laugh. Although Austin usually makes me laugh about myself in a way that makes me feel good. All the silly fantasies aside, I really like being around him. His foot brushes mine again as he takes a bite of his fries. Picking up my sandwich, I savour the feelings, the laughter, the warmth. I sense a subtle peace and belonging slowly setting inside me.

I could get used to this. Then I chuckle at my own stupid

cliche. *Who couldn't get used to a man like Austin?*

He picks up a napkin, and his face is oddly serious for a moment. "Actually, I was hoping you could give me some advice about school for Lily. She's really self-conscious about reading."

"Because of her dyslexia?" I ask.

Austin's eyes widen. "She told you?"

"No. Mari shared that. Lily didn't want to talk about it."

"That sounds about right. Anyway, her teacher is having kids read aloud in class. So far, she's dodged that bullet, but eventually it's going to come up."

"This can't be the first time Lily's had to read in school," I say.

"Well, no. She always finds a way around it or out of it. Mari helps her study at home. Lena would help her, too, but she really needs to find a way to participate. What I'm more worried about is a scene in class. Lily embarrasses easily, and I don't want her to go through that."

"Has she talked to her teacher?"

"I doubt it. Lily thinks she can keep it a secret as long as she passes the test. Which she will. She's very smart. Just listening to what the other kids say in class, she'll pick up enough to pass."

"She is obviously very smart," I agree. The approving smile from Austin momentarily distracts me, and I have to be firm with my mind before it leads me into another fantasy. "If she were in my class, I wouldn't want to embarrass her, but class participation is important. First things first, she needs to talk to her teacher."

"I agree, but I can't make her."

"No, but you could schedule a meeting to have that discussion together. Perhaps it's not mandatory for her to read aloud as long as she participates in the discussions. If it is mandatory, maybe she can decide with her teacher a passage to read aloud ahead of time so she can practise."

"Recite instead of read?"

"Well, sort of, but she doesn't have to memorize it. She'll

still have the book in front of her in case she gets stuck. Shouldn't her dyslexia be a part of her learning plan in school? Her teacher should be aware, right?"

"She is, but it's not the same for everybody, and Lily doesn't usually ask for any help. You wouldn't know any stubborn women like that, would you?" Austin asks with a wicked grin.

I shake my head, keeping a straight face. "I have no idea what you're talking about."

"Good," he says, leaning closer. "Then we shouldn't have any problems tomorrow."

Hanging my head, I shake with laughter. It feels good to laugh. When I look up, Austin's expression is pure amusement.

"I can ask for help. Thank you very much." I quip.

"We'll see about that," he says, laughing.

"Can I get you anything else?" the waitress asks.

I look up, surprised I didn't notice her walking over. "I'm okay. Thank you."

"No, she's not," Austin says.

"Excuse me?" I try to sound annoyed, but I'm already laughing.

"She needs pie," he tells the waitress, not looking at me.

He holds up two fingers. She nods and walks back into the kitchen. I'm staring at Austin as his beautiful smile meets mine.

"You need pie," he says, nodding confidently.

"Oh, yeah? I know just where to put it, too."

We both start laughing at the same time. It's no use trying to act serious around him. Before we finish the last of our food, two enormous slices of chocolate pie land on the table, the whipped cream so high it's toppling over. My eyes nearly tear up at the delicious sight.

"Told you," Austin says, scooping up a spoonful of whipped cream.
I nod and pull my plate closer. "Okay. You win. I need pie."

We dig in, and before I know it, my stomach and cheeks hurt from laughing so much. A little whipped cream may have gone astray as I retaliate against Austin's wicked wit, but I can't remember the last time I've enjoyed myself this much. Scraping the last bit of chocolate from the plate, I look up at the clock with the spoon in my mouth.

"Is it really 9 p.m.?" I mumble over the spoon. I slide it out of my mouth as I realize that we've been chatting for almost three hours. "What time do you have to be home for the girls?"

"Oh, shit. About twenty minutes ago. I'm surprised they haven't texted me yet," Austin says as he pulls his phone out of his pocket. "They did. I'm sorry."

I'm not sure who he's apologizing to. Austin taps out a message, then slides his phone back into his pocket and stands. Pulling out his wallet, he drops some cash on the table.

"They have keys to let themselves in, but I don't usually leave them alone for this long, especially at night. I've gotta run." He pulls on his jacket. "I had a really good time, though. Thanks for the advice about Lily. I'll see you tomorrow. Eight okay?"

"Yeah," I nod. "I'll be up."

I give a little wave as he turns and exits the diner. Then I look down at the cash he left. It's more than enough to cover both our meals plus a generous tip.

"Tomorrow," I say softly.

The waitress walks over with the cheque, and I pass her the money.

"Keep the change," I tell her, and pull on my coat. As I walk out of the dinner, my thoughts are all mixed up and incredibly focused at the same time. "Tomorrow."

Chapter 10 - Austin

I left before Charlie showed up. She called to say she was running late, and Mari was still asleep. I felt a little guilty leaving the girls alone to go see Sarah, but after I suggested to Lily last night that we have a parent-teacher conference, she wasn't exactly speaking to me. I know Sarah is right, though. As a parent, it's my job to help them learn how to face the tough stuff. If I don't teach her now, Lily will never learn to speak up for herself.

Breathing a heavy sigh, I pull out onto the road. It's a short drive to Lena's cottage. Which doesn't leave me much time for reflection. On the other hand, I know what's waiting for me and I can't wait to get started. I don't see Sarah as I pull alongside the cottage. Fortunately, there's plenty of room for my truck to drive straight to the back of the property. As I remove the straps from the skid steer, my phone chimes with a text from Charlie saying she's got the girls.

I message back just to touch base. Then I decide to message each of my girls. They get annoyed when I tell them I love them in front of their friends, or anybody, but they'll let me text it to them all day long.

Mari's response makes me laugh.

Mari: Love you too Dad. Can I have extra on my allowance if I talk Lily into responding.

Austin: Sure. If you'll spend an extra afternoon at the store this week.

Mari: Can I pick the day?

Austin: Nope.

Lily responds before Mari can finish negotiating.

Lily: Love you.

It's enough for now. I slip my phone back into my pocket and drive the skid steer off the trailer. My mind turns to pie and a pair of deep brown eyes. She favours Lena in more ways than one, but Sarah's laugh is something special, something completely unique to her. Walking towards the cottage, I examine the garden beds. She has been hard at work.

As my mind drifts over our conversation from the night before, I turn the corner to the cottage, lost in thought. That's when I smash directly into Sarah. Our bodies collide in such a way that I lose track of my hands and feet. A moment later, we're tumbling to the ground, where she lands straddling my lap. Her hands are pressed to my chest, and everything in me responds.

"Sarah! Are you okay?"

"I'm okay! I'm so sorry." She jumps back, landing on her butt, her face beet red.

I shake off the wave of sensations threatening to humiliate me. "No, I'm sorry. I was just parking the truck, and I- Here, let me help you."

Standing, I reach for her hands. Sarah doesn't make eye contact but holds her hands up. I lift her easily, holding her steady when she's back on her feet.

"Are you okay?" I ask again.

Her brown eyes come up to meet mine, and I see the corners of her lips start to twitch. I can't help it. I burst out laughing. Her giggling turns into a full on cackle as we begin brushing dirt off one another. It takes a few minutes for either of us to regain our composure.

When the dust finally settles, Sarah looks up and grins. "Good morning!" she chimes.

Rubbing a hand across my forehead, I chuckle. "Good

morning, Sarah. How are you today?" I ask with a mock-serious tone.

"Great, until some guy pushed me down!"

"Uh, I think 'pulled you down' would be more accurate, and that was an accident."

Sarah turns, rolling her eyes, and takes a step towards the orchard. "Pulled, pushed, either way it's a bad sign for my Blackeyes Susans."

I turn to walk beside her. "See, that's why you need to be the one steering. I'm obviously a safety hazard. The garden is much safer with you behind the controls."

Sarah's wide eyes glance my way. "Don't you mean 'behind the wheel'?"

"Not in a skid steer," I say, pursing my lips.

"Oh, geeze. Well, before we find new ways for me to kill myself, tell me what you think of this guy." Sarah stops in front of a pear tree in the center of the orchard.

It's slightly smaller than the trees around it, though by the looks of the trunk, I guess it was planted around the same time. I take a few steps closer, seeing the wilt at the ends of many branches. Still, there is some new growth. My mind shifts gears, and I walk slowly around the tree, examining the decay.

"Maybe if we put our heads together, we can rescue this broken heart," I say, laying my hand on the bark.

I stare up into the branches and wonder if I'm really talking about the tree or myself. Small, green leaves push out around buds near the top, and I feel like this pear tree, trying not to wilt with the loss. I miss Jenifer, more than I can ever express. I never felt guilty for dating, but no woman ever came close to touching the hurt of losing my wife.

"What do you think?" Sarah asks softly.

I look down to see her right next to me. Today, she's wearing overalls instead of the flowing skirts she normally wears. A handkerchief pushes her dark hair away from her face, making her brown eyes stand out more than usual.

If ever there was a woman...

I shake off the errant thought and return my focus to the pear tree. No sense in idle fantasies.

"I think I know what the problem is. You see how crowded the spurs are and how many are growing into the trunk?"

"Yeah. Several of the trees look kind of bushy like that," Sarah says, looking over at the ones closest to us.

"Well, that prevents light and air circulation. Since this tree is slightly smaller and close to its neighbours, I think it's just struggling to breathe."

"Really?" She leans in to stare up at the same leaves as me.

"It's probably a good idea to do some serious pruning all around, but I'd wait until after the first frost for most of them. We can get this guy cleaned up now since he's not producing much fruit anyway. Actually, it would be best to pick the buds so it can focus on growth this season."

"Okay. I'll go get the ladder." Sarah turns to leave.

I put a hand on her shoulder, stopping her dead in her tracks. As she turns to face me, I feel drawn to her lips. Suddenly, I've forgotten why I stopped her in the first place. We stand still like that for a long, cool minute with my hand still on her shoulder.

Sarah's eyes search mine. "What is it?" she asks, her voice soft and breathy.

My phone goes off, breaking the moment. "Sorry," I say. Mari's name appears on the screen as I unlock it. "Yeah, sweetheart?"

Another bid for extra spending money ends with both girls coming to the store for two afternoons this week. Sarah's attention wanders. I watch her out of the corner of my eye until Mari finally says, "Fine. Love you!"

The phone beeps in my ear before I can respond. "I love you, too," I mumble under my breath.

Sarah is walking away now, and I can only imagine what she thinks. *Does she know how close I came to kissing her for no apparent reason?*

"Sarah! Wait," I call, jogging to catch up with her. "I'm

sorry about that. They're apparently in the middle of spending my retirement on clothes for the summer."

Her laughter eases my fear that I might have made her uncomfortable.

"Maybe you should put them on payroll. Then at least you could deduct the cost of their wardrobe as salary," she offers, turning to smile at me.

"Right, but before you grab the ladder…" I point to the skid steer waiting at the back of the cottage.

"No, oh no. I don't think so. That doesn't even have wheels. Those things are like a tank tire. Do they call them tires with the flat, moving do-hickeys on them?" She's got both hands on her hips and is shaking her head.

As she starts to back away, I get behind her and put a hand on both her shoulders, gently nudging her forward. "You can do this," I encourage. "I'll be right here with you the whole time."

"With me, or run over?" she asks, giving in.

"With you, I hope. But…" I pause to help her into the cage. "If you manage to run me over, I have a life insurance policy that should cover Lily's college through grad school and maybe six months of Mari's shopping."

Sarah's eyes scan the cab. "There are a lot of buttons in here."

"Yup." I fold the safety bars down over her lap and point to the joysticks on either side. "These are the most important. This side controls the tracks."

"The what?"

"The flat, moving do-hickeys." I can't stop myself from laughing as I use her terminology. "This side controls the bucket. Up, down, tilt forward, tilt back."

Sarah watches me closely as I explain, but her expression seems less and less certain. I continue anyway, confident she can do this. Either way, I want to see her try.

"Ignition here. Unlock the hydraulics here, then release the parking brake. You ready?"

"No! Are you kidding me! You do it. Show me." She's

already pushed the safety bars up and is climbing out of the seat.

Blocking her way, I grin. "No, ma'am."

"But, but- Okay, can you sit in here with me?" she asks.

The cab is a tight fit for me. I can't imagine us both fitting in here. *Sarah is kind of short.* "Only if you want to sit in my lap."

She looks around the cab, then back at me. "I really would feel better, at least until I get the hang of it."

I nod, trying to quell my growing interest in this plan. I know I need to check that feeling or things could get very awkward very fast. Clearing my throat, I step back and help her out of the seat. We trade places, and she climbs in, making herself comfortable and me very uncomfortable.

Deep breaths, man, I tell myself as I lower the safety controls. I prop my chin on Sarah's shoulder to see around her. Her scent is intoxicating. I can't place it, but I inhale another whiff.

"Ready?" I ask.

Sarah just nods.

"You have to hit the buttons, remember? Ignition." I say, pointing.

Following my instructions, she gets everything ready and squeals when we begin moving. Her laughter continues as we roll over the site for her greenhouse. I show her a few things but I intentionally don't move a lot of dirt so she can do it. I want her to see that she can.

"Your turn," I say, setting the bucket down.

I imagine she'll put me out now, but Sarah slowly takes the controls without getting up and tests out the joysticks. She hits the forward hard, and the skid steer lurches.

"Ah!" Sarah screams as she lets go of the controls.

I pat her thighs, the only safe body part I can reach. "Don't worry. We're not going to tip over. First, ease the bucket up, then move around a bit until you get comfortable with how it responds."

"You're sure we won't tip over?" she asks, turning to look at me.

"Yes," I say, smiling. "Now, go on, before I'm old and grey."

"You're already a little grey," she says.

I huff a laugh. "Thanks for pointing that out. Now, get your butt in gear."

That retort is rewarded with her wiggling around until I feel like I could scream. "Okay! Okay! I'm sorry. You win!" I yell.

Sarah's laughter rings out, but she does finally move the skid steer. Just as I suspected, she's a natural. From my less-than-comfortable, but enjoyable spot, I talk her through grading the site for her geodome. Before I realize, my arms are around her waist. Sarah doesn't pay me any attention as far as I can tell, and I find myself wondering what would happen if I did kiss her?

Chapter 11 - Sarah

Duke nods as I slide onto a barstool a few seats down from him. I smile politely, but in the back of my mind, I wonder where his family is or if he has a family. The thought is short-lived as Charlie comes busting through the door from the Sandbar's kitchen. She's carrying half a dozen mugs and one wine glass.

"So, Sarah, big plans this evening?" Charlie asks as she lines the mugs up on the bar. "A little birdie tells me you have a hot date with a Moore brother tonight."

"You mean a couple of chicks told you we're going to the drive-in movies," I answer. "It's not a date. The girls like having me around, and I enjoy their company."

Charlie scoffs a laugh. "Whatever. I saw how cozy you two were when I dropped the girls off on Sunday."

"We weren't…" I shake my head, feeling a warmth creep up my neck as I remember sitting in Austin's lap on the skid steer. I never did let him go. We just kept working until we were done. He was comfortable. I was comfortable.

"Uh-huh," Charlie says. She's leaning on her elbows, watching me with a grin on her face. "For the record, Austin is one of the best guys I know. I wouldn't encourage you if I didn't trust him."

I roll my eyes, shake my head, and fail to come up with an answer. "He's really nice," I say finally.

"And this nice guy asked you out," Charlie supplies.

"No, he invited me to hang out with the girls."

"Wow. Delusional much? You can't tell me you don't see

the way he looks at you. Austin's a great guy."

"Neither here nor there, my friend."

"Why?" she challenges.

"You know why. I'm..." I lean forward to whisper, even though Duke doesn't seem to care. "...going to have a baby. I've almost got enough saved for the fertility treatments, and that's just too complicated."

Charlie folds her hands on the bar between us. Her silence weighs on me. She's my biggest supporter in my new life. If she gives up on me, I don't know what I'll do.

"Charlie?" I say softly.

She sighs before answering. "Maybe he'd be more understanding than you think."

I didn't expect that answer. For a moment, I chew on her words, but my mind takes me back to Frank. He should have understood. He had every reason to understand, but my ex-husband left me with no choice. *You have a choice,* I hear him say in the back of my mind.

"I left Frank for this," I say. Charlie knows the whole story. She doesn't need more of an explanation, but I give it anyway. "I didn't get divorced just so I could convince some other man that having a baby is important to me."

Charlie holds up her hands in surrender. "Since you're just friends, maybe he'll understand."

I shrug. "That's not the kind of thing you just tell people."

"I know. I'm just-" Charlie's lips twist over to one side. "Let's put a pin in that thought."

Charlie turns around and grabs two tumblers off a shelf. Pouring a shot in each, she passes me one. "A toast. To friends."

Eyeing her suspiciously, I raise my glass. The amber liquid goes down smoothly.

"It's a good thing I can walk to the drive-in from here!" I say with a laugh.

Charlie smiles. "Good point." Then she pours me another.

"So, this is your plan? Get me drunk and pass me off to your attractive brother-in-law?" I ask.

"Maybe," Charlie's grin turns maniacal. "So, you think he's hot?"

"New subject!" I sing.

Charlie slaps the bar. "Fine. I got you a present."

As she disappears into the back, I take a sip of my drink. I'm feeling the effects already, but there's time for coffee before I go to meet Austin and the girls. I laugh as I imagine Charlie playing matchmaker. *If only I could return the favour.*

She reappears with a reusable shopping bag, setting it on the bar in front of me before planting her hands on her hips. I pull out a light wooden square that looks like wall art. Turning it over, I see flowers and script painted across the front.

I read aloud, "*To plant a garden is to believe in tomorrow.* It's beautiful," I say, sniffing back a tear. "Thank you."

"You're welcome. For the record, Lily picked it out, but she asked me to give it to you."

I pull my head back, surprised that Lily would pick something out for me. "Why?"

"She likes you. You've obviously made a good impression on her. She needs a woman to look up to."

"Lily already has an amazing Aunt Charlie," I say, giving her a pointed look.

She smiles. "But you're different."

"You mean I'm shy like her?"

"You said it, not me," Charlie says, laughing. She turns to grab the phone off the wall as it rings. "Sandbar!"

The flowers on the small picture in my hand remind me of Black Eyed Susans or possibly Dahlias. I haven't touched the flower beds yet. *Maybe Lily will help me weed them.*

I *was* always the shy one, following in Charlie's wake as she took on the world. I can kind of see that with Lily and Mari. Knowing that Lily is a Moore makes me smile. Noah and William did a lot to draw me out of my shell as a teenager. *They're a good family.*

Charlie slams the phone down as a couple of guys find a seat at a nearby table. She winks at me as she darts past to take their order. Within a few minutes, another group comes in. I sip my drink, thinking about our conversation. Maybe Austin would understand, but a relationship would be much too complicated. I know what I want, what I've sacrificed, and I'm not giving up now.

With the Sandbar filling up, I decide to make my way to the drive-in. I catch Charlie for a quick hug as she steps around the bar with a plate of food.

"See you later," I say.

"You better," she answers, smiling as always. "Call me later."

"Yup." I hold my gift close as I walk to the door.

Outside, the warm summer air is refreshing. After dropping the picture off in my car, I walk to the ice cream shop. I like Ida a lot. I still haven't quite figured her out, but she has me pegged. Before I make it through the door, she has a cup sitting on the counter waiting for me.

"What did I get today?" I ask.

"Chocolate and coffee ice cream, topped with caramel," Ida says as she hands me a spoon.

The first bite makes me want to cry. It's so good.

"How did you know?" I ask with my eyes closed, savoring the flavor.

Ida laughs. "Well, you seemed serious as you walked this way."

Opening my eyes, I study her for a moment, but the woman remains an enigma. "Serious ice cream, huh?"

"As serious as ice cream can get. You want to talk about it?"

"No," I say softly. "Maybe some other time."

"Sure. My door is always open."

I reach for my wallet, but she shakes her head.

"Are you sure I can't pay for this? This is very rich, must be expensive," I joke just before stuffing another spoonful in my mouth.

"Let's just say I owed Lena a few scoops that I never got to repay her. It's part of your inheritance. I'll let you know when you run out of freebies." Ida's gaze drops for just a moment. Then her smile returns. "She was a wonderful woman."

"Thank you. I miss her."

"Me too." Ida's attention shifts as a family enters with two elementary-age kids rushing to press their noses to the glass.

"Thanks," I say, holding up my half-eaten ice cream.

Ida nods, then greets the newcomers. I take my cue and head back out into the soft light of the setting sun. I try to savor my dessert, but it doesn't last long. I toss the empty cup into the trash can outside the drive-in parking lot. Austin said he'd bring chairs and snacks, so I didn't bring anything with me.

I wander around for a bit until I spot Mari in a bright pink mid-drift that I'm sure is making Austin crazy. As I get closer, Lily and Mari spot me. Both come to meet me on the way to give me half a hug each.

"Hey, girls! How are you?"

"Great. Do you like my new shirt?" Mari asks. "Dad hates it," she adds, rolling her eyes.

I chuckle despite my best efforts. "It might be a little short for me," I admit. "But you look beautiful. You too, Lily. Is this new?"

She shakes her head. "No, I didn't find anything I like. Aunt Charlie says we can go to Barrie next week to shop."

"That sounds fun."

"You want to come?" Mari asks.

"Sure, I'd love to."

As we get closer, Austin stands. My heart flutters and knows that I feel more than friendship. His arms come around me in a quick hug, and the fluttering turns into a contest between my racing pulse and the butterflies in my stomach.

"You must have been to see Ida," Austin says as we sit down.

I feel my eyes widen with surprise. "How did you know that?"

He offers me a paper towel and points to my chin. "Because you have chocolate on your face."

"We should have gotten ice cream," Mari says.

Lily nods. "That does sound good."

While they continue to chat, my eyes meet Austin's. His broad smile warms me down to my toes.

Chapter 12 - Sarah

Inside Out plays on the big screen while Lily and Mari sit on either side of me, leaning in to reach the bag of popcorn in my lap. Austin came prepared: chairs, blankets, drinks, snacks. There's even a beach umbrella folded up behind his cooler in case of light rain. He never ceases to impress me with the lengths he'll go to for his girls. He's always making sure they get everything they need, even if it's just happy childhood memories.

Mari waves at another girl who looks about the same age as her family walks by. "Hey, Destiny!"

The girl sets down the lawn chair she's carrying to wave, then continues on. Osage holds so many happy memories for me. Spending every summer here with Zia Lena, Charlie, Zach, William, and Noah helped me become the woman I am today. I'm glad that Mari and Lily will grow up here, too.

My conversation with Charlie pops into my head, and I think about having a baby and raising them here. I smile as I imagine a baby playing in the soft dirt of the garden bed. Sure, it would be nice to raise that baby with someone as thoughtful and kind as Austin, but I can't say that's going to happen.

As my thoughts begin to turn blue like the memories the cartoon character, *Sadness*, touches, I try to focus on the movie. I want the bright, bubbly character *Joy* to be in control of my brain all the time.

Another girl stops to hug Mari on her way from the small concession stand at the back of the park.

"I'm sitting with Destiny. Come see us, okay?" she says.

Mari nods. "Okay. We'll come over at intermission." She glances at Lily, who smiles like she means it, even though the girl seems to be only talking to Mari.

Yup, just like Charlie and me, I think.

The blue feelings return, as I watch the memories being thrown into the chasm in the movie. I feel truly sad, both for the things I've forgotten and the things I can't forget. I imagine *Sadness* standing at the controls in my mind. Then Austin smiles at me, and I sense another emotion, one they don't cover in the movie. I can't explain what it is about him that makes me feel like we've been friends for decades rather than weeks.

By the time the credits roll, I've managed to rein in my emotions. I'm not sure how much Charlie's talk helped. It just got me thinking about things that I've been avoiding. Hurt that I can't ignore for much longer.

"Can we come over on Sunday?" Lily asks, as she stands.

I look up and realize Mari is already walking away, probably to find their friends. The crowds around us are all standing, taking advantage of the intermission before the second movie starts. The warmer weather has already begun attracting tourists to Osage Beach, but I recognize a few faces from around town.

"Sure, Lily. I'd like that." I start to say more about the flower beds in front of the cottage, but she's off before I get my thoughts together.

"I'll be right back," Austin says.

"Okay," I answer.

He leaves in the direction of the washrooms. Rather than let my mind revert to a past I can't change, I decide to take in the evening around me. Stars twinkle brightly despite the lights around the park. Standing, I stretch my back. Then I look for something to keep busy. Mari left a few napkins in her seat. Finding an empty bag, I tuck them and a few food wrappers away to toss later.

"Where's Dad?" Lily's face appears in my peripheral vision.

"I believe he went to the washroom. He said he'll be back in a minute."

Mari appears next with one of their friends in tow. "Did you ask?"

"Dad's not here," Lily answers, pointing to his empty chair.

Mari plops down next to me. "When will he be back?"

"When will who be back?" Austin asks, walking up.

"Can we go stay with Destiny and Becky? They're having a sleepover?" Mari says quickly, hopping to her feet.

Austin looks at Lily, who nods in response.

"Please, Dad?" she asks.

Austin looks from daughter to daughter again, assessing the situation. "Are you staying at Destiny's or Becky's?"

"Destiny's," the three girls say at the same time.

"You're just going to leave Sarah?" Austin asks. "She came to watch the movie with you."

His tone is playful, and I wonder if he knows how much I enjoy being with him.

Mari turns to me, slapping her hands together in a mock pleading. "Sarah, can we go hang out with our friends, please!"

"Sure," I say, chuckling. "I'll see you Sunday."

Lily and Mari are off in a flash. Without a moment's hesitation, Austin picks up his chair and sets it right next to mine. "Finally, I can get to the popcorn," he says, grabbing a handful.

"You're amazing with them," I say.

Austin shrugs like he might blow off the compliment, but then he looks directly at me. "They're the only thing that matters, you know?"

I nod, taking in another layer of Austin Moore. He's too good to be true, and yet here he is.

If only I had known when we were younger. It's a foolish thought. Who knows where we'd all be if one thing were different here or there? *Would Austin have stuck by me if I lost his baby?* Another foolish thought. I shake off the nonsense and focus on the here and now.

"Really, though," I say softly. "I would like to think I'd raise my children like you. Those girls are lucky to have such a great dad."

"I didn't start out this way. I've had a lot of help: my mom and dad, Ida, Lena. Especially as the girls got older. They spent a lot of time at the cottage. I did too after my mom passed away. She and Lena were close."

"They were." I smile, remembering her with Mrs. Moore. "They had a special friendship."

"Your aunt was so proud of you," Austin says. "She used to talk about you all the time. She thought you'd make a great mom."

"Zia Lena was always my biggest fan. I guess we all need one."

"True," he says, taking another handful of popcorn. "Can I ask why you don't have children?"

The question throws me for a loop. Austin has no way of knowing, and Zia Lena wouldn't have told him. I have to answer, though, as much as it pains me. I hope Charlie is right, that he'll understand.

I clear my throat. "I have a son."

"You do?" he asks, looking as confused as I would expect him to be.

I nod. "He passed away before he was born."

Austin's arms come around my shoulders. I can't return the embrace without throwing the popcorn down, so I just lean into him.

"I'm so sorry," he whispers. Then he lets go. One arm stays comfortably around my shoulders. "I had no idea."

I make a pitiful attempt at holding back the tears, but my cheeks are wet in an instant. "It's not really a secret. It's just not the sort of thing you tell people you don't know. I, um-"

"I'm glad you told me," Austin says, gently rubbing my shoulder.

I'm glad I told him, too. Charlie was right, but deep down I already knew he'd understand. "It's nice to acknowledge him even if it's just me that misses him."

Austin squeezes my shoulder, pulling me closer to him. "Do you want to tell me about him, about what happened?"

I hesitate for a moment, and then under Austin's calm stare, I dive in. "One day, around thirty-five weeks, I noticed that I hadn't felt the baby kick for a while, so I sat down to measure kick counts. It's a thing you're supposed to do every day, count how many kicks you feel in an hour-long period, and if you get to ten, the baby is moving around plenty."

"I remember Jennifer doing that," Austin says softly.

"Well, that day, I didn't feel any, even after sitting still. I tried having some juice which encourages movement, still nothing. I called my midwife and met her at the hospital for an ultrasound." My tears flow freely now. I have to stop talking to breathe. It's been so long since I've told this story, and I feel every word as a sharp pain in my chest.

Austin sits quietly beside me. His demeanor remains steady, comforting. I'm grateful for his friendship.

Wiping a few tears away, I continue. "When they couldn't find a heartbeat, they told me to call my husband. When he arrived, they confirmed our baby had passed. I was in complete shock. I had trouble understanding what they were saying, but the gist of it was that they didn't know why this happened. He was just gone."

"I can't imagine," Austin says, rubbing his beard thoughtfully with his free hand. His other arm remains around me. His kind eyes meet mine. "What happened next?"

"I think that was the hardest part. The doctors said the safest thing to do was to induce labour. I had to deliver a baby that was never going to live." I feel my head shaking at the thought, but I'm as disconnected from the moment now as I was then. "I don't remember much from that day. After he was born, a kind nurse helped us take pictures to remember Sprout. That's what we called him while he grew in my belly. When he died before we met him-"

My words trail off. Even four years later, this is still so hard. My eyes flit up to the big screen as the colourful emotions move about *Headquarters.* I watch absentmindedly for a moment before my focus returns.

"I know it's a bit of a non-traditional name, but Sprout just seemed to fit when I saw him. On the twenty-first, it will have been four years since his Angelversary. That's what the day is called by those who have stillbirths. And I still think about him every day, but it's hardest on that day."

As painful as it was to share my heartache, I feel better having talked about my baby boy. No one can know him like I did. The eight months we shared together were something so special. At least now I can talk about him with someone new, someone who understands what it's like to lose a loved one.

"When I'm visited by butterflies, I always think of him."

Chapter 13 - Austin

"Butterflies?" I ask, curious about the connection. When I asked Sarah about having children, I never expected her to answer the way she did. My heart aches, and I feel for her, but I also feel guilty. My mind keeps going back to Jennifer, of leaving the hospital without my wife. On the other hand, I feel like I understand Sarah's pain in a sense because of our shared loss.

"Those first few days were the hardest," she says after a long pause. "I had just given birth, and my body was not my own, but I didn't have the baby to show for it. I remember going to the mall to buy clothes for the memorial service. I was certain that people around me could tell I had just had a baby, but I had no baby with me. In my mind, I was already making up excuses, lies to tell people so they wouldn't judge me. I felt guilt and shame for losing Sprout the way I did."

"You know you couldn't control any of that, right?" I ask, quietly.

Sarah nods. "I know it was wrong. I just couldn't help it."

For a moment, her tears fall faster. All I can do is sit with her, help her to feel safe in her grief. I know that all too well. A part of me wants to find a way to protect her from the pain, but I know it's too late for that. Even if I had been there, like with Jenifer, there's nothing that would have stopped the avalanche of hurt.

Passing her a bottle of water and a napkin is all I can do. Sarah accepts both, with a grateful look.

"Thank you," she says, trying to smile. "The next month

or so was a blur of grief. Then I had to go back to work like nothing ever happened. Looking back, I can see how very broken I was. I don't know how I made it through. But the butterflies helped. That spring and summer, in my garden, I was visited by monarch butterflies – way more than usual. I started to think of butterflies as Sprout keeping me company when I gardened. Is that silly?"

I'm surprised Sarah would ask that, but I get it. I clear my throat as I try to find the words. It's been a long time since I talked about losing my wife. I talk to her picture on the wall every day. I tell my girls stories about their mom every chance I get, but not about that awful time right after I lost her.

"No, it's not silly," I say, still floundering in my thoughts. "When my wife died in childbirth, I couldn't comprehend it. Like, my brain just would not accept that she was gone. It didn't feel real leaving the hospital without her. Even after the funeral, I kept expecting to wake up and find her next to me. Weeks went by, and I went through the motions. Thank God for my girls. They kept me going. One day, when the girls were a little over a month old, I walked past Jennifer's picture hanging on the wall while carrying Mari. She smiled, like a great, big 'Hey, I know you' smile. I kind of thought it was a fluke, probably gas. Then later that day, Lily did the same thing. It was like they knew she was there, watching over us. I still talk to that picture every day."

I laugh, suddenly caught up in a memory. "One time, Mari was mad at me and told me I was a bad Dad. She was only five or six years old. I was pretty upset with her, but I can't for the life of me remember why. I told her, 'Oh yeah? Go tell someone else you're mad, because I don't care.' Mari stormed out, and I instantly felt awful. I went after her and found her looking up at that picture of her mom, telling her exactly why I was a bad Dad. I loved it."

"That's beautiful," Sarah says.

A gentle smile greets me when I look down at her. I can feel my heart begin to beat a bit faster, but I don't dwell on it. My mind is on Jennifer, and I'm glad to be able to share my love for her after all this time.

"I still catch the girls talking to her sometimes. I guess they've seen me do it enough." I shake my head, feeling both happy and sad. "I can't imagine going through life without my girls. I am so sorry for your loss, Sarah."

"Thank you."

Simple and honest, just what I've come to expect from her. Sarah's tears have slowed, and we both take a deep breath. Shifting in my chair, I notice my leg has fallen asleep.

"Since the girls have abandoned us, why don't we go for a walk?"

"What about your stuff?" Sarah asks, looking around.

"No one's going to bother it, except maybe the girls. I'll text them and tell them where we're going."

A moment later, we're picking our way through the crowd to the back of the park. The beach is a short walk from the drive-in and I head that way. Sarah walks alongside me now that we're out of the way of the moviegoers. The warm summer night is peaceful. A waning moon sheds just enough light on our path that we can easily meander without tripping over anything.

"That's why it ended. Between me and Frank," Sarah says when we're well out of earshot of anyone else. "He didn't understand. I needed to be a mom."

"What do you mean?" I ask.

We walk along the beach for a while before she answers. "We decided to try again, but month after month, nothing happened. Frank knew I was still grieving, and he was willing to try to have another baby, but he never understood the intensity of my need. I guess he didn't feel the same. After a year, I suggested fertility treatments. At first, he was resistant, but we discussed it. I went ahead and got checked out. When I knew I wasn't the problem, I brought it up again. Frank refused to get tested. He said we didn't need fertility treatments, that if it was meant to be, it would happen. End of discussion."

"Yikes," I mutter.

Sarah nods. "That pretty much ended all discussion

between us. I couldn't accept that answer. Discussions turned to arguments, and after a couple years, I gave up. I decided if I couldn't have a baby with him, then I needed to go it alone."

"That's why you're here, isn't it?" I ask.

"Yes. I've been saving money for fertility. Living in Zia Lena's place saves me on rent. A couple of months or so, and I'll have enough to get started."

"Plus, Osage is a great place to raise children," I offer.

"That too. You don't think I'm wrong for going this alone?"

"I think wrong would be the wrong word." I laugh at myself, at my mastery of language.

Sarah chuckles too, but I can tell she's not laughing at me. It's so easy to be around her, to talk to her. I place my hand on her forearm and we stop walking.

"I think you'll be a great mom, Sarah." I bend to catch her eyes with my own.

"I hope so," she says with a sigh.

We continue to walk and chat, but the conversation shifts to less meaningful aspects of life in Osage. Further down the beach, I spot Sarah's car parked under the streetlight at the Sandbar. Our feet move that way. When we get there, we're still talking, and we lean against her trunk.

In the blink of an eye, a sharp whistle rings out. Sarah and I turn to see Charlie walking across the otherwise empty parking lot. I have the strange feeling of getting busted, not that I mind getting caught with Sarah, but I feel like a teenager getting busted with their girlfriend after curfew.

"Where're the twins?" Charlie asks as she walks up, grinning, her eyes bouncing between Sarah and me.

"Sleepover with a couple friends," I answer.

Charlie's shoulders slump. "Aw, I was gonna kidnap them for my own sleepover."

"You can come over to the cottage," Sarah offers. "I'm up for a sleepover and I have cookie dough."

"You just got yourself a sleepover," Charlie says, pointing a finger and smiling.

It's good to see her smiling, really smiling. I worry that my sister-in-law has spent more time masking her own hurt than dealing with it. I glance between her and Sarah.

"I guess I should head back," I say.

"I could drive you back," Sarah says quickly.

Charlie elbows me. "Good idea! I'll meet you at the cottage."

Subtle.

Sarah unlocks her car, and we both get in. Before the engine is warm, our conversation flows naturally again. When she drops me off, I realize how much I miss having an adult to talk to, someone not macho and competitive like my brothers. I always miss my daughters when they're not at home, but I'm glad tonight worked out the way it did. The more time I spend with Sarah, the more I appreciate her presence.

Chapter 14 - Austin

On Sunday, I decide to go to Sarah's with the girls even though they don't want me to. I realize they're growing up and looking for independence. It's not that I mind that. Whether I'm ready to admit it or not, I want to see Sarah again. So, we all check our bike tires together.

Once they've got helmets on, I strap a Bergamot plant into each of the girls' bike baskets. The purple flowers are nearly too tall for Mari and Lily to see over, but they don't complain.

"You ready?" I ask.

Lily starts pedaling.

"Meet you there!" Mari calls over her shoulder as she catches up with her sister.

I exercise my patience and give them their head start. Letting them grow up is the hardest part, but I know it will happen either way. Counting to twenty, slowly, I feel my chest tighten the farther away they get. Then, I get on my bike and follow.

By the time I reach Sarah's, she is standing with the girls examining the flowers. Her brown eyes meet mine.

"They attract pollinators," I say, not sure how she'll react. I want her to know why I brought them from the store, but I don't want her to be uncomfortable in front of the girls.

Sarah's eyes grow glassy for just a moment. She nods at me, then turns her attention to Lily and Mari. "Why don't you girls help me pick a spot for these? They like filtered light, right, Austin?"

"You are correct."

"What's filtered light?" Mari asks.

My twins each have a pot in their arms as they begin walking next to Sarah.

"That means in a spot where the sun won't shine on them directly, but they still get lots of light." Sarah moves towards the cottage.

Realizing that I hadn't dismounted my bike yet, I set the kickstand. Rather than follow the girls and rain on their independence, I decide to make myself useful. In the lean-to, I find a shovel and a trowel and carry both to the girls.

"I'm going to remeasure the space for the greenhouse. The supplies are in. I just want to make sure I've got everything right."

"I really appreciate it," Sarah says, smiling at me. I love the way her eyes crinkle with her smile, even when her lips don't curve very much.

"What are you looking at?" Lily asks, swinging her head between me and Sarah.

"Nothing. Excuse me." Scratching at my neck, I make an awkward exit.

There is nothing that really needs my attention at the site for the greenhouse. I measured everything carefully before I placed the order. Still, I need to give the girls space. I walk the outside perimeter of the grading.

Sarah did an excellent job. I could use her for advertising. A YouTube video of her operating some of the heavy equipment might encourage other women to take a chance. She has enough space. I might be able to convince her to install a small pond, an excellent project for the micro excavator.

I can't help chuckling to myself as I walk back around to the front of Sarah's cottage. Helping her grade for her greenhouse is the most fun I've had in a long time. Mari pats the dirt around one bush while Lily carefully measures her hole in the ground. Lily takes a few more scoops out before gently brushing the roots at the base to loosen them.

"Great job, Lily. Where did you learn to do that?" Sarah

asks.

My beautiful girl glances up at me. "From Dad. He loves plants."

"That, I do," I admit proudly. Catching a glimpse of Mari out of the corner of my eye, I take a large step back. The precocious one has the water hose in one hand and the nozzle in the other. I can tell it's on by the drops of water dripping from the closed nozzle.

"Sarah, can you come here?" I say, emphasizing my nervousness.

Her eyebrows furrow as she quickly stands and walks towards me. I admire how her skirt sways with her hips, but when she reaches me, I grab her shoulders and spin her around.

"Hide me!" I say, ducking behind her as best I can.

Sarah lets out a peal of laughter as Mari opens the hose, watering in the plants and her sister in one fell swoop. I stumble backwards, tugging Sarah away from the impending water fight.

Lily marches straight towards Mari, hands out, grasping for the hose. "My turn!" she shouts.

Sarah and I watch the melee from a safe distance. Within minutes, Lily and Mari are soaked through. As their tug-of-war continues, I sneak around and cut off the water hose.

Squeals are replaced with "Aww!"

"I think the bergamot is well watered," Sarah chimes. "Let's check on our seedlings."

After we checked on the raised garden beds, we spent some time pruning the struggling pear tree. I admire how easily Sarah splits her attention between my girls. Both Lily and Mari are all smiles for hours as we work. I wonder how much they really enjoy gardening or if it's more about having a woman to look up to.

I can't help but think how nice it could be to have Sarah as a more permanent part of our lives. Before I can even consider exploring that option, I remember our conversation at the drive-in. Sarah knows exactly what she wants, and it doesn't involve dating.

Maybe I'm ready to start dating, I think as I put the ladder away. The idea leaves a bad taste in my mouth when I remember the last woman I went out with. *Maybe we're all better off with a friend like Sarah.* I walk back to find the three of them laughing and talking.

"Dad, can we have dinner with Sarah tonight?" Mari asks.

"I don't think so." I shake my head as I look over my lovely girls, caked in mud from head to toe. "I think we should go home and get cleaned up."

"But you're not dirty," Lily says.

My eyebrows lift in question. "What's your point, sweetheart?"

"Lily's right, Dad," Mari piles on. "We'll ride home and change and come right back. You can stay here with Sarah and order the pizza."

"Or, the three of us could go home and come back in my truck," I suggest. I know where this is going -- doing things on their own.

"Dad, we'll be right back," Mari argues, climbing on her bike. "Okay?"

I cave, reluctantly. "Right back. If I don't see you back here in thirty minutes-"

"We need to get cleaned up, Dad. Remember?" Mari says, rolling her eyes dramatically.

"Forty-five minutes then. That's ten minutes there, ten minutes back, and twenty-five for showers. Lily, use my shower so you don't have to wait on each other, okay?"

Lily nods as she pushes off, following Mari, who's already pedaling away. I run a hand through my hair as I watch them go.

"Good job, Dad," Sarah says.

"Don't laugh at me!" I retort, pointing at her smirk. "Wait until it's your eleven-year-old and see how you feel about it."

"Do you really think it will happen?"

"What?"

"That I'll have my own one day?"

"Of course it will." When Sarah's eyes turn glassy, I pull

her into a hug. "And I'll be a good friend and not laugh at you when you have a hard time letting them do things on their own."

Sarah chuckles at that remark. I know she'll be alright, and she'll be a great mom. The hug lingers longer than I planned.

"Well," I say, as I pull away. "What kind of pizza do you like?"

"Supreme. You?" Sarah asks.

We walk inside her cottage, discussing the merits of pizza toppings. I can't stand them, but I joke about ordering anchovies just to see Sarah's nose wrinkle up.

"If you do, you're eating that pizza outside," she says, laughing.

I end up ordering a supreme and a half cheese-half pepperoni for the girls to share. When the pizza shows up before they do, I start to worry. I text Mari, but get no response. I text Lily, nothing.

"It's only been thirty minutes," Sarah says.

I give her a mock mean look as I call Mari's phone. Sarah laughs and shakes her head. I love that she gets my sense of humor. Then I realize that I hear Mari's ringtone. We both look over to see two cell phones on her kitchen table. I end the call and start towards the door.

"Wait, *Dad*," Sarah says, picking up her keys. "I want a Diet Coke. Do you have any left over from the movie?"

"Yeah." I draw out the word, studying her. I swallow hard against my dry throat while my heart gallops in my chest from not knowing where my girls are, but I wait to see what she has in mind.

"I don't feel like going to the store. Mind if I pick the drinks up from your house?"

"You don't have to do that."

"Sure, I do. I'm thirsty. I'll text you as soon as I see them and they'll never know you're a worrywart."

"They might already know," I say as she walks out the door.

I pace the floor, but not for long. Sarah sends me a text a

few minutes after she leaves, telling me the girls just got out of the shower.

I breathe a sigh of relief and mumble, "Thank you, Sarah."

She texts me fifteen minutes later to say the girls are going to ride back with her. Assured that my girls are perfectly safe and probably not going to be annoyed with me for checking on them, I peruse Lena's bookshelf. Besides a few science books, I see that Sarah has kept most of Lena's books just the way they were. Lena always appreciated a good book.

I pick up a dusty copy of L'Amour and relax on the couch. As the girls walk in, I'm sure I look perfectly content, but Lily is on to me.

She plops on the couch next to me and whispers, "Thanks for sending Sarah." Then she hops up to follow her sister into the kitchen.

Shaking my head, I can't help but smile. The twins are so different. Lily is the sweet one. Mari is the confident one. As evidenced when she finds her phone, turns on her music, and begins dancing around the kitchen like we're at a club, not a quiet cottage at the edge of town.

"Nice moves, Mari!" Sarah cheers her on.

Lily joins in, and the two of them coax Sarah into dancing too.

"You've got to hold your arms like this," Mari says, teaching Sarah the moves.

I set the book down and walk over to the kitchen. I plan on turning the music down, but the song changes to something quieter. Mari grabs my hand and pulls me towards the tile floor. Thinking that she wants me to dance with her, I follow, but she pushes me towards Sarah. Then Mari grabs Lily and the two begin waltzing around the kitchen, making circles around us.

I shrug my shoulders. "Care to dance?" I ask.

To my surprise, Sarah shrugs and holds her arms out. Stepping closer, I can feel heat on my neck. I'm sure I'm turning red, but having my arms around Sarah quickly shifts my focus.

She's smiling as her brown eyes gaze into mine.

"Thanks for being a good sport," I say, leaning in to whisper.

She simply nods, and I'm drawn to her soft lips. My eyes linger, and I'm leaning closer. The music suddenly changes to a raucous clanging that I'm not even sure is music. The girls begin jumping and bouncing around.

"Excuse me," I say to Sarah. I find Mari's phone and cut off the noise.

"Aww!" the twins say at the same time.

"Pizza's getting cold," I answer.

Everyone's attention diverts to dinner. I can feel my pulse racing. Another second, and I would have kissed Sarah. I glance her way, and I think I see her blushing. I want to kiss her, but I don't know where that would lead. I'm not interested in casual dating.

I find myself wondering all through dinner what Sarah is interested in, relationship-wise. Can she see anything beyond becoming a mom? Could she see herself with me, with my girls?

Chapter 15 - Sarah

Mid-morning on May 21st, the anniversary of the day I lost my Baby Sprout, I'm standing in front of my washroom mirror, pensive. Dabbing at my eyes, I'm glad Austin invited me out with him and the girls. I will be thinking about Sprout all day, but at least Austin knows. It'll be good not to spend the whole day with nothing to occupy my mind. Pinching my cheeks, I try to balance out the splotches from crying when I hear a knock on the door. The knock is followed by the sound of Mari's voice.

"Sarah doesn't mind. She said we're welcome anytime."

Mari's voice is chased by Austin's. "Welcome doesn't mean let yourself in, Mari. Get back here. Lily!"

"It's fine," I call as I round the corner.

Lily sits in her favourite spot by the window facing the orchard. Mari is rummaging through a cabinet in the kitchen.

"If you're looking for cookies, I'm afraid you're out of luck," I say to Mari with the best smile I can muster.

I'm glad she feels welcome, but today is Sprout's angelversary and there's only so much I can do to hide my broken heart.

Austin stands in the doorway, looking slightly irritated. His broad frame takes up nearly the whole entryway. "I'm so sorry," he says, shaking his head.

I don't bother answering him. I need a Moore hug, so I walk straight to him and wrap my arms around his waist. Austin hugs me back, and I feel everything turn upside-down. If the day wasn't what it was, I might over-analyze that feeling. Instead, I welcome the distraction.

"It's fine," I whisper. "Come in."

As he steps inside, the topsy-turvy feelings flip again. I'm happy he's here. I'm happy the girls are here. I miss my baby boy. I miss Zia Lena. I still think of this as her cottage, not mine. Maybe I should take notes from the girls on making myself at home.

"There're graham crackers in the pantry, Mari," I call over my shoulder as I close the door behind Austin. "Thank you for inviting me to tag along," I tell him.

His smile derails me. "No problem. I'm glad you can come. It'll be nice to have back up."

Austin and Mari exchange looks. Hers is sassy and dismissive, while Austin's is pointed. I sense a battle over clothing style is already underway. Amused, I smile at Mari.

"I'm sure we can find something your dad likes."

She shrugs as she pulls a few graham crackers out of the box. "Good luck with that."

"So, are you ready for a day at the mall?" Austin's voice has a hint of sarcasm.

My smile is more natural as I pick up my purse. "I'm ready. Are you ready?"

"No, but here we go." He slaps his hands, rubbing them together. "Girls!"

Mari manages to beat us all out the door and into Austin's truck. Austin opens the door for me and helps me up. I'm glad he has running boards, or I might not have made it into his large pickup. Lily and Mari hop in like it's no effort at all.

The hour and a half drive to Vaughan, the suburb of Toronto, includes a lot of singing and laughter. Mari and Lily are great company. Austin humors them by singing along with pop stars I know he has no interest in, and I admire that. He is a fantastic father. Occasionally, he slips in a few made up lyrics that the girls miss from the back seat. When he glances my way, I giggle at the expression he makes as he turns Taylor Swift's *Trouble* into a goofy mash up.

When the mall finally comes into view, I'm a little sad that the ride is over. I've had so much fun riding, singing, and chatting with the girls and Austin. Looking out across the mall parking lot, I can tell it's going to be crowded. There is a sea of cars. Austin stops short of the turn in, and I realize he's letting out the cars that have been waiting, stuck because of the red light. When three cars zip out, he makes the right-hand turn.

With kind gestures like that I can't imagine why a man like Austin is still single. My stomach turns a flip again, and I look out the truck window to hide my blushing. I shouldn't be thinking about that. I *can't* think about that. Austin is a great guy, but I have plans. Many long hours of thought and tough decisions went into me moving to Osage. As great as Austin is, I don't have room in my life for chances right now.

"Can we get a pretzel? I'm so hungry!" Lily says as three doors to the truck pop open.

I unbuckle my seatbelt, still a little lost in my thoughts.

"I could go for a pretzel," Austin says. He opens my door, greeting me with that warm smile I've come to look for. Holding my hand, Austin helps me down, still chatting with the twins. "Both of you have your phones on you, right?"

"Yes," Mari says, rolling her eyes.

Lily nods as she taps her screen. I wonder who she might be texting. Austin's phone dings.

"Good. Both fully charged?" he asks, showing me a message from Lily with the eye roll emoji. "Don't forget where the truck is. If we get separated for any reason, you will call me and we'll meet at this entrance, right, girls?"

"Yeah, Dad. Come on!" Mari grabs Austin's hand and tugs him towards the mall.

Lily falls into step next to me. "What are you going to shop for?"

"Um," I shrug my shoulders. I hadn't really thought about shopping. "I'm not sure. What are you going to buy?"

"A new bathing suit," Lily says. She tucks her phone in her pocket and smiles up at me. She has her dad's smile, and I imagine her mom's eyes.

The combination makes me wonder what my baby might look like. Will they have my eyes or someone else's, some donor I've never met?

"I might get my hair cut," Lily adds.

"Really? I love your hair," I say.

"Yeah, it's just kind of long. Are you going to swim at the beach with us?"

"When?" I remember Charlie mentioning a beach day, but I thought that was just the two of us.

Lily nods. "Weekend after next, May two-four. Uncle Noah is getting his boat out. It'll be fun. You should come."

"Okay. I guess I should get a bathing suit, too." I shudder at the thought of Austin seeing me in my old, worn-out suit, but the idea makes me chuckle too.

William Moore started calling me *sexy ass Sarah* when Charlie caught him staring at us one beach day, years ago. I knew all along who he'd really been staring at, but I'd been sworn to secrecy already. So, we went with it. When I called him on it later, William said the name still fit even if I wasn't the sexy ass he happened to be staring at.

I have so many good memories of spending my summers in Osage with the Moores and Charlie. A beach day with all of them sounds like a great way to spend the holiday. I haven't gotten to spend nearly as much time as I'd like terrorizing Noah anyway. I miss him, but Charlie says he and William stay busy with their rental business.

"Dad, Sarah needs a bathing suit, too. Can we go there first?" Lily asks as we walk into the mall.

I know I'm blushing when Austin glances back at me. "Sure, honey. Right after pretzels."

Swimsuit shopping goes surprisingly smoothly. Mari's two-piece is a little skimpy, but she picked out some shorts to go with it. Lily went with a one-piece and a nice wrap. I, on the other hand, end up with a two-piece that doesn't cover nearly as much skin as I'd like. High-waisted black bottoms and a polka dot blue and black bra-like top, Mari goaded me into trying it on.

I did it just to humor her, but Austin's expression as I walked out of the dressing room made me buy it.

Charlie's going to have a field day when she sees this. I hold the shopping bag close, like I'm afraid someone will see what I have inside.

"Dad, can we go to Claire's?" Mari asks. She and Lily are already walking that way. Austin glances at me.

"Sure," he says to Mari. "Sarah and I will wait here."

"See you!" Mari calls as she and Lily walk faster, anxious to get away.

I wait next to Austin as he watches them go. When Mari and Lily step inside the store, he turns slowly to face me.

"Sorry," he says, letting his head dip. "I'm trying to give them their space, but it's hard. They're my babies."

"You're doing great, Dad," I tease, elbowing him in the side. We wait on the bench outside the store. The girls are easy to spot through the window displays. When they finally come out, I stand and nod across the way. "Come on. I need a raincoat."

LL Bean is a short walk from Claire's. The girls peruse the funky sock arrangement, as I try on coats and Austin tries on hats. Most of them are funny things he would never wear, but he pulls on a blue ball cap, and I stop to stare.

"You should get that," I say, admiring how the navy brings out the colour of his eyes.

"You think so?" Austin pulls it off and spins it backward. "Do you like it?"

"Yes," I say dreamily.

"So, it's comfortable?" he asks.

I finally realize that he's asking about the coat in my hands, not the ball cap. "Oh, this, no. Um, maybe the first one I tried."

Putting the second one back, I pick up the first coat and slip it on. "What do you think?"

Austin rubs his chin thoughtfully. Then he steps closer and buttons the coat, tying the belt loosely. He steps back and gives me the once-over. "I like it."

Heat creeps up my neck. "Okay," I say softly. "I guess I'll take this one."

"What took you so long?" Lily asks as we walk over to the twins, who are admiring the sunglasses display.

"My fault," I say, holding up my new coat. "Tough decision."

Mari and Lily both admire the rain jacket. It wasn't a tough decision at all. I start to think that Austin's smile could decide just about anything for me. I reign in that thought as best I can, but I can feel my convictions slipping away.

"Well, I'm hungry," I say to distract myself. "What are we going to eat?"

"How about pizza?" Mari suggests.

"How about Chinese?" Lily says.

"How about, it's a food court. Everyone picks what they like,"" Austin says. After purchasing the coat and ball cap, we make our way to the food court. Austin hands each of the girls a twenty dollar bill. "Stay where we can see you."

Lily and Mari are off in a flash, leaving their shopping bags on the table.

"What about you?" Austin asks, quirking a brow over one of those blue eyes.

"Um, I could go for a sandwich," I suggest, turning to face the deli behind us.

Austin sets his shopping bags in a chair beside. "Great idea. You want to hang out here, guard the swag, and I'll grab us some food?"

"Sure. Roast beef, please."

Austin returns with two sandwiches and a slice of pie for us to share. While we eat, Lily and Mari talk about the haircuts they want to get and the stores they want to see next. Austin sits next to me with an arm stretched across my chair back. I consciously try not to lean into him, but I want to. I want this, to be with him and to have a family. As wonderful as Lily and Mari are, I'm not ready to give up my dream of having a baby of my own. As my thoughts weigh on me, I sigh.

"Everything okay?" Austin asks.

"Yup, just full, I think," I lean back and enjoy the feel of his arm around me.

Austin smiles. "I hope you're not too full. I can't eat this alone."

He pushes the pie container closer to me.

"Maybe just a bite."

The rich chocolate tastes amazing, and I end up eating more than my fair share. When we all finish our food, our next stop is the hair salon. While Lily and Mari get their hair cut, I step over to the coffee shop and get a chai tea.

"I'm glad you came," Austin says, sitting on the bench next to me outside the salon.

"Me too. This has been fun." I sip my tea and for a moment, the rich aroma carries me away, but the place I normally escape to in my mind is now my home. I miss Zia Lena so much. Being able to stay in her cottage is more than a dream come true.

"Here they come," Austin says under his breath.

Mari walks out with a mature bob cut, much too short for Austin's taste, I gather by his forced smile. Lily's hair is still long with some nice layers added in.

"You both look beautiful," I say.

Austin nods. "Yes, you do."

"Thanks, Sarah!" Mari spins around. "Do you really like it?"

"I love it." I stand and tug on Austin's arm. "Let's go pick out a nice outfit to go with it."

Chapter 16 - Austin

Mari walks out of the dressing room in short shorts and a crop top that barely classifies as a top at all. I'm shaking my head "no" while my daughter glares at me defiantly.

"Sarah, you like it, right?"

I'm ready to put a stop to the madness when Sarah steps in front of me.

"I love that purple. So pretty. Here. Try it with these jeans," Sarah says, passing Mari a pair of blue jeans.

"Whose side are you on?" I mutter as she turns around.

Mari smiles and walks back into the dressing room. Lily comes out in clothes that are actually tasteful, and I wish with all my heart that Mari took after her sister more in this one area.

"Just," Sarah puts a hand on my arm. "See it with the jeans, okay."

She turns to see what Lily has on. Lily managed to find a tank top that covers her waist and shorts that almost come down to her knees. Why Mari can't find a single outfit that covers this much skin, I don't know.

"You look great, Lily!" Sarah cheers. "I love those colours."

The stripes on Lily's tank top alternate between shades of green. A moment too late, I realize I've been silently brooding. Lily's expression falls.

"You look wonderful, honey," I say. "I'm sorry. I was distracted."

Lily nods, but I worry that I missed the moment with

her. That happens more than I'd like. Mari's bold personality takes up a lot of space, especially when it comes to her wardrobe.

"What else have you got to try on?" I ask, hoping for a second chance.

Lily walks back into the dressing room, passing Mari on her way out. The blue jeans Sarah gave her are high-rise, a style from the eighties that I can say I was glad to miss the first time. On the other hand, the waistline is so high, the crop top almost reaches the denim.

"What do you think?" Sarah asks with a beautiful smile.

Mari beams at her. "I love it! Do you like it?"

"Oh yeah," Sarah says. "Dad, what do you think?"

"I think that is acceptable, but those shorts are going back."

"Fine," Mari scoffs, barely suppressing the eye roll.

As she walks away, Sarah grins at me.

"Okay," I huff. "That was a good call."

"You're welcome," she sings.

Lily appears, and her attention diverts again.

"Oooh, I like that!" Sarah says.

"Yes." I jump at the chance to cheer Lily on. "I love the colour. You look great, honey."

"Really?" she asks, looking up at me with big eyes that remind me so much of her mom.

"Absolutely," I say, smiling widely.

Lily's wardrobe is always a no-brainer, but sometimes I forget to show her how beautiful I think she is all the time. Mari comes back with her clothes, and I try not to be too obvious when I look to be sure the shorts were left behind. Sarah offers to carry her selections so Mari can carry the shopping bags from the other stores, and I notice her neatly arranging the clothes on her arm. She turns and winks at me.

"No shorts," she whispers as she walks towards the register.

I realize I need to take notes from Sarah. She's got a few tricks up her sleeve.

She'll be a great mom, I think. *If only...*

I stop myself before my mind goes down that road again. I've only been down that rabbit hole at least a hundred times today. Sarah and I could be great together, but could I give her what she really wants? If I can't, what then?

There's no use lying to myself. I didn't plan this whole day around Sarah because I just want to be friends. For now, that's all we are. That's all I can promise her. I understand her grief too well to ask her to change her plans.

"Earth to Dad!" Mari calls, shaking me out of my thoughts.

The cashier is still bagging up clothes, so I know I haven't drifted too far. I pass her my card as Lily and Mari scoop up their purchases.

"Aren't you forgetting something?" I say to the back of their heads.

"Thanks, Dad!" they call over their shoulders.

Sarah chuckles. Just for fun, I give her the side-eye. This makes her laugh harder. She nudges me, then follows the girls out. I catch up to her and take her bags.

"Thank you," she says. "This has been fun."

"I'm glad you enjoyed it. I'm not sure I can handle all the things getting shorter."

"Shorter?"

"Yeah, you know, haircuts, crop tops, shorts."

Sarah smiles at me. "For the record, I agree with you about the shorts, but I like her hair. It fits her personality."

"I guess you're right about that. I miss them being-" I hesitate to avoid saying the word *babies*. I don't want to put that thought into Sarah's mind. This day is hard enough. "Younger," I say instead.

"Younger children are less challenging in some ways, less independent, but I always get so excited when I see my students start to take chances. They start to show the amazing people they'll be someday, and I like to be a part of that... as a teacher, I mean."

"And one day, as a mom," I say encouragingly.

Sarah nods resolutely. "Yes."

"Will you keep teaching?"

"I think I'll have to. Childcare is expensive, and I'm on my own now. I'll have to work."

Our conversation is cut short as we reach my truck. I help Sarah into the cab, and I linger at her door as she buckles in. After a moment, she looks up at me. Her expression is pleasant but curious.

"If you're not in a hurry to get home, I think I'll take the scenic route."

"Sounds good to me," Sarah says.

"Great." I close her door carefully and walk around to the driver's side.

My girls are chatting away, indifferent to our route change, leaving Sarah and I to talk on our own. I couldn't find a better pair of daughters, but I'm more concerned with Sarah at the moment. I planned this day for her so that she could enjoy herself and hopefully not struggle. I also know that grief needs acknowledgement. She'll never forget her lost baby the same way I'll never forget Jennifer. I chose our next destination with that in mind.

As I drive, Sarah's arm rests on the center console between us. Resisting the urge to wrap my hand around her delicate fingers, I change radio stations. My girls protest, but I land on classic rock and turn the volume down to background noise level.

"I'm not sure I've been this way before," Sarah says, admiring the scenery.

"It's the long way home, but if you're really not in a rush, there's one more place I'd like to stop." I slow down for the turn before Sarah answers.

In her usual way, she's open to anything.

Add that to the list of things I like about her.

The two-story, glass building comes into view as we round a curve. The girls love the butterfly park. I've come here with them more times than I can count. This time of year, everything is in bloom in the surrounding gardens.

"This is beautiful!" Sarah says with a little gasp. "Where are we?"

"The butterfly gardens," Mari answers. "You've never been?"

Sarah's eyes land on me. I can see her staring out of my peripheral vision. After carefully pulling into the parking space, I look over at her.

"I bring the girls here all the time," I say quietly.

Mari and Lily are already out of the truck and walking towards the entrance. Sarah's wide eyes scan the surrounding gardens, then take in the building itself. I walk around to open her door and she's quiet as we walk in. I'm not sure what to say or do. So, I simply stay next to her, walking in step, hoping this was a good idea.

Lily holds the door open for us as we reach the building. Mari has disappeared, probably already in the butterfly garden. When Sarah hesitates in the lobby, Lily grabs her hand and begins walking to the hatchery.

"This is my favourite part!" Lily says with her hands pressed to the glass. She points to a cocoon that twitches near the back. "This one will hatch in a minute. Watch!"

Moments like this, I feel like my girls are still girls, little girls. I'm greedy for moments like this, but I keep an eye on Sarah for signs that she knows why we're here. She stands quietly next to Lily, watching obediently. The dark-blue butterfly cracks the shell open, and two antennae appear. Mari comes out of the inner garden to stand next to her sister.

"Oooh, he's almost out!" Mari whispers excitedly, tucking short strands of hair behind her ears.

Lily leans on Sarah's shoulder, pointing with her opposite arm. "There are the wings."

Standing behind them, I feel like a guard. While I make it my business to protect my girls, probably a little too carefully, I'm not sure Sarah would appreciate it. She's independent and tougher than she gives herself credit for.

The butterfly comes fully out of the cocoon, blue-black wings slicked against its body. It won't be long now before he's ready to fly. No matter how many times we watch it, the process still amazes me.

Another family crowds in, and I nudge Lily. "Let them see," I say, nodding to the younger children.

Lily moves away, pulling Sarah with her. "Come on," she says, tugging Sarah towards the door that Mari holds open.

I follow them into the butterfly garden, where the air is humid and warm even for summer. Butterflies dance everywhere across the two-story enclosure. Sarah's eyes scan the room following the movement of wings. Lily and Mari skip further into the garden, looking for their favourite plants.

"This is amazing," Sarah says. Her voice holds the sound of awe and wonder. "I can see why the girls love coming here. I've never seen so many butterflies."

When she faces me, I can see the tears she's fighting. I want to comfort her, but I hold back. There's a fine line between friends and something more, and I'm not sure I could control myself if I got too close. Especially, because I want to.

"Do you like it?" I ask.

Sarah doesn't answer me. We both watch as a large monarch butterfly flaps its wings slowly, gradually falling between us. Sarah lifts her hand, and he lights there, on her soft fingertips.

"It's like he knew you were coming," I say in a whisper.

Sarah swallows and nods. Her brown eyes come up to meet mine, and if not for the butterfly, I would cross that invisible line. Instead, I stand with her and watch as the beautiful wings flap lazily. When the monarch finally lifts off, Lily and Mari are there, waiting to show Sarah everything they love about the garden.

Chapter 17 - Sarah

A towel, sunscreen, hat, sunglasses, what else do I need? I hold my bag as I circle my bedroom again, trying to remember what I'm forgetting. My nerves have me twitching. I'm looking forward to hanging out with everyone, but... *Austin will be there.*

I stop and sigh at myself in the mirror. Running a hand through my hair to smooth it out, I resume my search. Austin and I have seen each other since the butterfly garden, but we haven't been alone. We haven't really talked.

Every night and half the day, I think back to the moment we watched the Monarch land on my finger. I felt closer to Sprout at that moment than I had in a very long time. When the butterfly took flight, I watched it soar up, high above my head. Then my eyes came back to Austin's, and he looked at me in such a gentle way. It felt like he was gauging my reaction to the special outing. I realized how much thought Austin put into planning that particular day for me on Sprout's angelversary.

Of course, I didn't get to ask him or say anything. Lily and Mari were there, ready to gobble up our attention. I enjoyed spending the day with them as well. Austin's girls are both so special. Just like their dad.

Charlie knocks on the door, and I give up my search for the missing item I cannot seem to identify.

"Wow! Look at you!" Charlie grins at my swimsuit.

"That's what I was looking for," I say more to myself. "Be right back."

Leaving my bag on the kitchen table, I retrieve the wrap

that I planned to wear over my bathing suit. I'm tying it around my waist as I walk back out of my bedroom. This bathing suit is a little out of my comfort zone, but the black high-waisted bottoms and structured blue top do flatter my body if I must admit it.

"We're going to have to beat the guys off with a stick when they see you in that."

"No, you won't," I say, shaking my head. "Besides, Austin and the girls already saw it. Mari helped pick it out."

Charlie's grin only widens. "Uh-huh. What about William? Has he seen it yet?"

"You know, Charlie, I don't think I'm really William's type." I know who is his type, but I don't know what he's waiting for.

"He's called you sexy ass Sarah since we were in high school. Is it that you can't take a hint, or are you too hung up on Austin to care?"

I force a smile. I don't want to change the subject. I want to ask Charlie why she can't take a hint? William is obviously still hung up on her. After this many years, she needs to let go of the past.

Like me?

"You know why I'm not dating anyone, not William, not Noah, not Austin. I've already made my first appointment at the fertility clinic."

Charlie's smile drops away. "You have?"

I try not to let her somber tone get to me. Picking up my bag, I walk towards the front door. Charlie follows. Once outside, I pull the cottage door closed behind us and check to be sure it's locked. Then I pick up our conversation.

"Appointments fill up fast. It's not until November."

Although the doctor I use is busy, I also don't quite have all the money saved up yet. Despite that, I'm confident that I'll be ready when the time comes.

"That's good." Charlie sounds chipper, almost convincing. She is still my biggest supporter, but she's been leaning more towards the start-a-new-relationship side of things. I hope that's a sign that she's considering finally moving on, but I've been nurturing that hope for a long time.

"Oh, wait," I say with a hand on Charlie's car door.

"What?" she calls after me as I dart back into the cottage.

"Boat snacks!" I yell over my shoulder.

I snatch up the second bag I left sitting on the kitchen table and head back out the door.

"Okay, ready!" I say as I plop down in Charlie's car.

We're laughing as she pulls down my driveway. It's been more than a few years since Charlie and I went out on a boat with the Moore brothers. I'm looking forward to the day with them.

...and Austin. I'm looking forward to seeing him, even if we won't get a chance to talk with all the people around.

Halfway there, Charlie takes a detour.

"Where're we going?" I ask.

"Picking up Lauren."

"Oh, cool. But, um, aren't we going out on Noah's boat?"

Charlie shrugs. "Yeah, and?"

"Oh, come on. There's clearly a lot of tension there. Will he even let her come?"

"He will if he knows what's good for him," Charlie says with an edge to her voice. "Besides, he doesn't say 'no' to me. I'm his favourite baby sister," she adds playfully.

"Right. So, what's the deal with her and Noah?"

"I think it's misplaced attraction."

"You think everything is misplaced attraction," I mutter.

"When the guys see you in that swimsuit, I don't think the attraction will be misplaced at all."

"Shut up," I snap in good humor.

Charlie just laughs.

To my surprise, Lauren and Noah simply ignore each other while everyone else exchanges greetings. Austin takes my bags from me to load them on the boat while Noah spins me around. My feet barely touch down before Mari and Lily are on either side of me, chatting up a storm. I do my best to follow their separate trains of thought, but I am distracted by Austin patting the seat next to him.

I take the seat and look up into his blue eyes, shaded by the cap he bought when we went shopping, and I can feel that quasi-lost feeling. All my plans, convictions, desires, everything melts away, leaving a single want. I want to know what it feels like to be in his arms. Not like we are now. Austin's arm rests on the seat behind me. His fingers lightly brush over my skin once, but I want more.

While the girls settle into their seats, my mind wonders if it was ever like this with my ex. We loved each other once, a long time ago, but I never felt so lost with him that I didn't want to be found. As I realize I'm comparing Frank and Austin, I stop myself. Austin and I aren't together. I'm just being silly.

Shifting my focus, I take a deep breath of the fresh air. Noah steers us smoothly out onto the lake. His pontoon boat is far nicer than the tiny boat we used to go out on as kids. Business must be good for him and William. Out of the corner of my eye, I see Charlie slide her cooler out.

"Oh, my favourite!" William says, reaching in to pull out an ice-cold beer. "Boat snacks!"

"Boat snacks?" Lauren asks, accepting the can he passes her. "What are boat snacks?"

I intercept Austin's beer and pop it open. "They're snacks you eat on a boat. Therefore..." I say, grinning.

"So, anything you eat on a boat, basically," Lauren says flatly.

"Yes, but you have to say it like you actually like snacks," William challenges, leaning over Charlie's shoulder. He looks like he's hoping to pilfer through her bag of chips and dips, and crackers, and cookies, but I know he's just enjoying the excuse to be close to her.

"If you brought a birthday cake on the boat, would it be a boat snack?" Mari asks.

Charlie nods with a mock-serious expression. "It's on the boat, it's boat snacks."

Lily starts to giggle. "What about a huge turkey leg?"

I laugh with her. "Yup, boat snack."

"I'm not sure I get it," Lauren says.

"You wouldn't," I hear Noah mutter.

I'm the only one who hears him, I think. Austin must have heard it, but ignores the comment. When I look up at Noah, he smiles widely at me. His light brown hair ruffles in the wind, and it's hard for me to imagine him not liking anyone.

Maybe Charlie's right with that misplaced attraction.

Out on the water, Noah sets anchor so everyone can swim. The water is deep, but the girls are great swimmers. They dive right in, followed by Charlie and William.

"You want me to help with that?" Austin asks, holding his hand out for my sunscreen.

"Sure," I say, passing it over.

I try not to let the feeling of his strong hands massaging my shoulders and back get to me, but it does. When he stops, I miss it instantly.

"What about you?" I say, turning to face him.

Austin pulls his shirt off, shifting in his seat. He has a bit of a dad bod, lovely broad shoulders, and a little hint of a stomach, but his smooth skin is flawless. I delicately rub sunscreen over his shoulders and cover his back. I know I'm blushing. Fortunately, most everyone is in the water already and not there to see me embarrass myself ogling Austin.

"Thanks," he says, standing.

I nod, averting my eyes. "Mm-hm."

As he walks to the side of the boat where everyone is swimming, I watch him go. Then I join Lauren to sunbathe on the front of the deck.

"So?" she asks as I lay down next to her.

I shake my head. "So?"

"Seriously, you two look awfully cozy, and he's not bad looking in those board shorts."

Both are hard to argue with. Austin does look good, and I enjoy being around him. Still, I shake my head. I decide to be open and honest with Lauren.

"I'm planning to start a family. I'm, um, I have an appointment for fertility services. I think that might be a deal breaker for dating."

"You might be surprised. I'm pretty sure he'd love to have more children," Lauren says.

Her confidence in that statement surprises me. We haven't gotten to know each other that well yet, but I imagine being close to Charlie means Lauren has spent time with Austin.

"What makes you say that?" I ask, watching him out in the water.

"My sister was in town a couple months ago with my niece. She was six weeks old at the time. When we went by the hardware store, Austin came around the counter, arms stretched out, offering to take the baby.

"Really?" I ask.

"Oh yeah." Lauren nods.

She turns over, propping up on her elbows, and I do the same.

"Austin didn't give the baby back until he walked us out to the car, twenty minutes later. My sister asked him if he wanted kids, and he told her about losing his wife when the twins were born. I didn't know how it happened until that conversation, but he said he felt like he missed so much of them being babies because of the grief."

"That's so sad," I say.

"It is. But he did say he'd wanted to have another baby so he could experience it all without the fog. I think he means it." Lauren gives me a pointed look.

"What?" I ask, a little confused.

She smirks. "He wants more kids. You want kids. So…"

I'm shaking my head, temporarily lost for an argument. It comes to me quickly enough. My ex wanted kids until he didn't anymore.

"I don't know," I say instead of unloading all that drama on Lauren.

I hear the sound of Austin's voice out on the water, and I want to think it could work out, even though I already know it won't.

Chapter 18: Austin

I swim closer to the boat when I hear my name. At least the part of the conversation where Lauren told Sarah, I "offered to take the baby." When I listened to her tell the story to Charlie last week, you'd think I tried to kidnap her niece. Truth be told, I feel guilty for wanting more children. At least I used to.

When Jennifer and I started trying to have a baby, at her insistence, I wasn't sure I was ready to be a dad. Of course, by the first ultrasound, I was a goner for my girls. But, surviving all that grief and pain left me with few memories of the little things, the smiles, them learning to make eye contact, the first time they rolled over on their own. It had been a long, hard road.

With all this running through my head, my eyes start to tear up as I reach for the boat ladder. Hoisting myself out of the water clears my head, but I walk past Sarah and Lauren to be sure I don't ruin their day with my brooding. I grab three beers out of Charlie's cooler and walk back. Passing one to Lauren, I sit next to Sarah and open the second can.

"What are you ladies talking about?" I ask, taking a sip.

The ice-cold beer feels good going down. Then I pass it to Sarah and open the last can. She's sitting up now, and I miss the view from a moment ago of her stretched out in that two-piece.

"You," Lauren says with a chuckle. "And my niece."

I nod, thoughtfully. "How is she?"

Sarah watches my expression. I should thank Lauren for bringing the subject up, but I'm not sure where this really leaves us. Sure, I want more children, but it's not a deal breaker for me.

For Sarah, it is, and I know it.

"Tammy is good. My sister says she watches her daddy everywhere he goes. She's pretty good at pushing up now, too."

"She'll be crawling before they know it," I say, smiling. It's genuine even though I struggle to remember that time in Mari and Lily's development. There's still so much they're learning to do, and I'm amazed every day at how independent and strong they both are.

An errant thought reminds me why Lauren's sister had stopped by the store. "Did Sarah tell you she's building a greenhouse? Next time your sister is in town, she should take a look at Sarah's and see if she likes the style."

"You have a greenhouse?" Lauren asks.

Sarah bobs her head. "Well, I will soon. I hope."

"We've got all the materials. Some assembly required, but Sarah already graded the site." I can't fight my wide grin remembering that day. I nudge Sarah's arm, and she laughs.

"You graded it yourself?" Lauren's smiling too, but she's on to me. She knows I'm bragging, and I'm pretty sure she knows why. "What did you use to grade? Also, what is grading?"

"Uh, honestly, I'm not really sure. I just know I needed a flat spot to build my geodome, and Austin brought over this big thing with tank wheels and made me drive it."

"Skid steer and you did great," I add. "Those wheels are called tracks, remember?"

Sarah's nose wrinkles up as she laughs again. "I was so nervous, but that part is done. Now, I just need to put it all together."

"I'll bring it all over next Sunday," I tell Sarah. "You can come help assemble it, if you want," I add to Lauren.

"No, you don't have to do that," Sarah says, shaking her head. She takes a long sip of her beer.

She's the shy one of the group.

Charlie and Mari are two of a kind, but Lily is my shy one. Lauren is more middle-of-the-road. She's easy-going, unless she's around Noah, but not as outgoing as Charlie by any stretch of the imagination. Charlie, like Mari, is nothing if not outgoing.

"If you're okay with it, I'd love to help," Lauren says. "My sister has been talking about building a greenhouse since before she got pregnant. Maybe I could help her get one put together before baby number two comes along." She quickly holds out a finger. "But don't tell anyone I said that. They're waiting to announce it."

"Already?" I ask.

Lauren nods. "Yeah, well. At least we know they're still happily married."

Sarah sits quietly, her focus on the beer can in her hands. I can see the hurt in her eyes, the sense of loss. The unwanted jealousy she feels when she finds out someone is having a baby, and she is not. Lauren doesn't seem to notice. She takes another long sip of her beer, then stands.

"I'm going to swim for a bit." Lauren quickly lowers herself down the ladder, and I hear her voice join the others in the water.

I'm torn between wanting to comfort Sarah and helping her just enjoy the day.

"Sorry," she says in a low voice, referring to her watering eyes.

Shaking my head, I lean my shoulder into hers. "No need. I get it."

A moment passes before Sarah's eyes meet mine. She attempts a smile. *That's my cue to move to another topic.*

I clear my throat dramatically. "So, I was thinking, I just added a new front loader to my inventory. If I could get a video of you using it in one of those flowy skirts you like so much, it'll be great for business. Encourage other ladies to try out the heavy machinery." My smirk is tentative until Sarah laughs.

She throws her head back and puts a hand over her eyes. "I don't even know what a front loader is!"

"No problem. I'd be happy to teach you how to use it. I really enjoyed showing you how to use the skid steer." I nudge her shoulder again for emphasis.

Sarah's cheeks turn red as she laughs harder. She rolls her head over to glare at me. "Why not have Charlie do a promo video?"

I frown and shake my head. "I am not letting Charlie sit in my lap."

"Why not?" Sarah challenges. Her smile is beautiful and playful.

Fighting to keep my face straight, my shoulders shake with the laughter dying to get out. "She's too tall."

"Too tall?" Sarah asks. "That's it?"

All I can do is grin. I wink at Sarah and lean my shoulder into hers again. She laughs and leans back into me. There is a long list of reasons why I would pick Sarah over Charlie any day. But that list isn't really what's important to me at the moment. The smile on Sarah's face is all I care about.

"Thanks, I needed a laugh," she says in that soft, sweet voice.

My heart rate kicks up a notch as I imagine hearing that voice, seeing that smile, when no one else is around. I swallow the knot that quickly forms in my throat. Then I try washing it down with beer. No denying it anymore. Sarah is what I want.

"Anytime," I say, my voice hoarse. I put an arm around her and pull her gently to my side. "Anytime."

"Girls, you ready?" I call down the hallway, checking the time again.

Lily appears first. She's wearing the outfit Sarah picked out for her, a green striped shirt and blue jeans. I smile as she walks towards me.

"Ready?" I ask, pulling her into a hug. Lily hugs me back and continues on.

Then Mari walks out of her room.

"No," I say, shaking my head. "No, Mari." I suck in a breath. *Gently,* I remind myself. *Save the force for when you really need it,*

because you're going to need it.
The challenge in my daughter's eyes is all I can take, but I temper my response.

"If you want to help with the power tools, you know the rule. Pants and no..." I gesture to the purple shirt that she got away with buying when Sarah was with us. "Mid-drifts. Try again."

Mari huffs and spins around. My hand involuntarily comes up to cover my eyes. I rub the crease in my forehead, knowing that she's the one who put it there, and wait. A few minutes later, Mari returns, still wearing the purple mid-drift, but she's put on overalls.

Close enough, I sigh. "Fine. Let's go."

I might have argued longer, but the whole Moore clan is waiting for us at the store, and we've got to beat the vacation traffic. On a sunny Sunday morning in May, the main streets will be clogged with city people trying to get to the beach from their rental cottage. Our town is not quite big enough to handle all those interested in our beach in the summer. Lily hands me a travel cup full of coffee when I walk in the kitchen.

"Thanks, honey," I say, giving her another half a hug.

Mari dashes by snatching my keys off the counter. "I'll start the truck!"

"E-brake!" I call after her.

Mari is gone, leaving Lily and I in her wake. Lily looks up at me and giggles at the look on my face.

"She gets it from Aunt Charlie," I say, trying my best to look amused rather than annoyed.

Lily just shrugs and walks out the door. I pause on my way out to look at the picture of Jennifer hanging on the wall. In my heart, I know she's happy for me. She was a lot more like Charlie than Sarah. Loud and confident and not at all reserved. But Jennifer would want me to move on, to be happy.

"I love you," I whisper to the picture. Then I walk out the door, my thoughts firmly planted on Sarah.

Chapter 19: Sarah

The sound of a truck coming up my driveway draws my attention away from breakfast. I'm so tired of eating Greek yogurt and granola. I just want a biscuit, a great big buttery biscuit. I sigh as I walk towards the door.

Nutrition is important for fertility.

Walking out onto my front porch, I see Austin's truck rolling past. Lily and Mari wave at me. I lift my hand to wave, but I feel my jaw dropping as I see the other two trucks coming. Connor nods curtly from the driver's seat of the second truck. Austin's hardware store logo is stamped on the side of both. The last one slows down, and Noah hangs an arm out the window.

"If it isn't Sarah the Terror on her own turf!" he says, bouncing his eyebrows at me.

William smiles from the passenger seat.

I chuckle. "Here to keep me out of trouble?"

"Here to get you in as deep as I can!" Noah half shouts as he pulls the truck past, following the other two.

I'm shaking my head and laughing as Charlie's car pulls up by the front porch.

"Hey!" she huffs as she darts past me into the cottage.

Lauren climbs out of the passenger side and approaches slowly, looking around. "This is nice."

"Thank you." We stand awkwardly for a moment. "Do you want to come in?" I ask, pointing a thumb at the front door Charlie left open. "I have hot water for tea."

"Sure," Lauren nods.

As we walk in, Charlie is walking out of the washroom.

"That was a close one! Traffic was such a mess! We should have just met everyone here. So-" Charlie plops down at the kitchen table. "Are you ready to build a greenhouse?"

"You- You're all-" I stammer. "I thought Austin was just bringing the supplies."

Charlie's smile is obnoxious. "Right. He's just going to drop all this off and say, 'Good luck, Sarah!' Like it or not, girl, he's got it bad. I can promise you."

"I think he's just being nice," I try. I shift my focus from Charlie to Lauren, but her expression is equally unconvincing. "He really didn't tell me anything."

Before Charlie or Lauren can laugh at me, Lily comes through the front door. "Hey, Sarah. I brought you some cookies."

"Thanks, Lily." I take the small container from her. "Did you make these?"

She nods and sits down next to Charlie. "Dad says we'll be here all day. Can we order pizza later?"

"Pizza sounds like a great idea, but we better order early to beat the tourist rush," Charlie says, running her fingers through Lily's long hair. "What are you going to work on today?"

She shrugs. "I don't know. Dad said we had to wear pants if we wanted to help with the power tools, though."

Lily looks me over. I glance down at my skirt, imagining it getting tangled up in something. "I guess I better go change then."

I can hear Lauren, Charlie, and Lily chatting indistinctly as I rummage through my dresser. I'm sure what I'm looking for is right in front of me, but I can't focus on anything. My mind keeps shifting between Austin's blue eyes, the fertility appointment card taped to my fridge, and the skid steer. Or rather, the feeling of Austin's arms around me as I drove the skid steer.

My hands latch onto denim, and I pull it out before I forget what I'm doing here. As I slip into the overalls, I remember the last time I wore them, the day we graded the site for the geodome. That was also the day I managed to land in Austin's lap in my front yard. Running into him like that was an accident, but when I got there, straddling his body, I felt things I hadn't felt in a long time. With my heart fluttering, I drop the snaps twice.

"Oh, you're in trouble," I tell my reflection.

Managing to pull myself together, I walk out into the kitchen. "Where's Mari?" I ask, hoping no one notices my lack of composure.

"She's outside with Dad," Lily says. "He gave her the supply list."

"I guess we should get out there." Charlie stands. "Wouldn't want her to have all the fun without us."

As we file out the front door, I'm again stunned by the number of people and tools in my yard. Connor, Noah, William, Austin, and Mari are all busy. Mari holds a clipboard and is giving her uncles direction while Austin loosens the straps off the trailer attached to his truck.

I decide to head straight to the mastermind, but as I walk towards Austin, a strong pair of arms snatch me up. I'm laughing and gasping for air as Noah runs me like a football the last few yards to where Austin stands.

"I got her!" Noah yells. "Here she is! Ready to work."

I land with a thump, and Noah's hands are planted firmly on my hips to steady me.

"Let me go," I say, laughing and pushing his hands away, a little embarrassed.

Noah laughs and pats my shoulders, massaging them gently. "Fine. What else can I get into?"

Austin's frown is more convincing than usual. His voice holds an edge. "Can you help Mari sort the plexiglass pieces? She has the inventory list."

"She has help," Noah gripes.

Lauren stands next to Mari, reading over the list. Noah's glare is ominous.

"Oh, get over yourself and go help your niece," Connor

barks. He walks past us carrying a table saw, not slowing down to argue.

Noah pats my shoulder one more time. "Killjoy." Then he walks over to Mari and Lauren.

Austin's eyes roam over me as he props an elbow on the bed of his truck. Before he can say anything, William walks up.

"So," William says flatly.

"Lily wants to learn how to use the table saw," Austin says. "What about you, Charlie?"

I turn to see her walking up behind me. Charlie slaps her hands together. "Yeah, table saw!"

"There you go. Do not leave Lily alone—"

"With a table saw?" William asks, wide eyed and clearly annoyed.

"I was going to say, 'alone with Charlie' but that's probably wise too," Austin says with a smirk.

"Come on." Charlie grabs William's arm.

As she drags him away, Austin winks at me.

He knows! I'm tempted to ask him just how much he knows about how William feels about Charlie, but Noah's back already.

"Seriously, any other job but—"

"Uncle Noah?" Mari calls.

Noah hangs his head. "Fine, but you owe me."

"For what?" Connor scoffs, walking back to the truck. "Get back to work."

"Hey," Austin says softly, stepping closer to me. His arms wrap around my shoulders, and I melt into him. "Would you mind fixing some tea and lemonade for later? Dad's bringing lunch for everyone."

"You didn't have to do all this," I say with my head lying on his chest.

"Sure, I did," Austin says. "I hope you don't mind."

"Depends. Does this mean I have to drive more heavy equipment?" I ask, ready to give him a hard time.

"You bet it does," he says, but as Austin steps back, his

smile captivates me.

    I press my lips together, but I can't help but smile. "Fine."

Chapter 20: Austin

As Sarah walks away, Noah grabs her arm to whisper something in her ear. I want to strangle him.

"Would you just go help your niece?" I yell at my brother.

Noah gives me a dirty look. "Fine. Tyrant."

I watch him squeeze Sarah's hand before trudging back to where Lauren and Mari are separating the plexiglass.

Connor shakes his head. "I know he's a pain in the ass, but you know he's not interested in Sarah. If I were you, I'd be more worried about William. He sure was eager to come today."

I glance at William for appearances, but as usual, his interest is firmly planted on Charlie. "Yeah, I guess."

"You know," Connor pauses as we lift the first ten-by-six out of my truck. "Neither would be a problem if you'd hurry up and make your move already."

"You're one to talk," I shoot back.

"You want me to put the moves on Sarah?" He says it with a straight face, but I know my brother. Connor's cheek twitches ever so slightly, like he might actually smile for once.

I shake my head as we set the board down and walk back to my truck for a second one. "Anyone else, literally anyone else. Pick any other living, breathing female in Osage, and make a move."

Connor huffs, which for him passes for a laugh. "I know what the problem is."

I am afraid to know what he thinks my problem is, but as I have corralled him on his day off, I humor him with a response. "What's that?"

"It's been a while. You're afraid little Austin won't be able to stand at attention."

And now I want to kill Connor. I spit and sputter for a moment while he grins. "You know what, if my daughters overheard that, you're explaining what that means," I say with my eyes darting between Lily and Mari, praying they didn't hear any of it.

"They're in the sixth grade. They probably already know what it means," Connor dead pans.

If we weren't in the middle of moving several hundred pounds worth of wood, I might take this moment to start a real fight with my big brother.

"New subject," I nearly shout.

With a shrug, Connor picks up the next board. "How's Eric working out?"

"Great. Fantastic, actually. You didn't tell me he was an athlete. First new guy who's been able to outlift me in a long time."

Connor's eyes narrow on me. "What kind of scrawny kids are you hiring?"

"What's that supposed to mean?" I ask with a threatening edge to my voice. A lot of damn good it does me.

"It means you're not exactly in top shape yourself there, *Dad*."

Just to prove a point, I pick up three boards this time. Connor lifts the other end like they weigh nothing. One side of his cheek twitches again, and I know he finds my feeble attempt at being macho funny as hell.

"Whatever, asshole," I mumble.

"You're not in charge here," I hear Noah bark. "Mari is."

"Yeah, well, Mari said to do it this way, or weren't you paying attention to that?" Lauren's voice is only slightly sharp, meaning they aren't really fighting, yet.

I look around to see Mari making her way back to the plexiglass from the cottage, with Sarah following behind.

Good. She can referee this time.

Connor shakes his head. "I know she's Charlie's friend, but does she have to come to every family event? I'm really getting sick of listening to them go back and forth."

"Me too," I say as we walk back for the last of the wood. "But she *is* Charlie's friend."

More than once, I've considered locking Noah and Lauren in a closet together. Either they come out dead, or Charlie's right, and they finally admit they like each other. I'm okay with whichever happens first.

And then there's the other twin to worry about. I look over at William. The years he's spent pining away for Charlie are almost as pathetic as Noah's stupid ego. William looks like he's picking up a chick at a pool table the way he's leaning over Charlie, holding her hands in place.

I shake my head, unwilling to play matchmaker for either of my brothers. I have my own problem, and at the moment she's walking my way.

"Hey," I say, trying not to sound out of breath from the last few loads of wood.

Briefly, Connor steps between Sarah and me. "You mind if I step inside?"

"Not at all," she answers with a wide smile.

As he moves past her, Connor turns to give me a pointed look. I grimace and shake my head. I know he means well, but he also doesn't know the whole story.

Conversation for another day.

"So," I say, clapping my hands together. "Ready to build a greenhouse?"

Sarah nods, but her smile is even brighter. I love seeing her this way, so happy and confident.

"While William, Lily, and Charlie finish cutting the wood for the base, how about you and I start laying out the plexiglass around the site in the order we'll install it. I think Mari's helpers have finished unloading it," I say the last part with a little bounce of my eyebrows. Noah and Lauren are still arguing, but

Mari snaps her fingers, and the two are cut off.

"Listen, guys. Do I need to separate you two?" Mari asks.

I must have said it one too many times because she sounds just like me. Sarah's shoulders shake, even though she tries not to laugh out loud.

"Sorry, Mari," Lauren and Noah say, nearly in sync.

"Good," she says. "Now, to the next truck."

Mari points, and Noah and Lauren dutifully walk past us to start unpacking more supplies. The way she lords over them with her clipboard makes me proud as hell. Selfishly, I want to teach her to run the hardware store, but I know she's too good for that. Whatever Mari decides to pursue as her career, she'll be great at it, and I'm sure it will be something like a lawyer or a doctor. At least I'll have help for a few summers in between her taking over the world.

Lily walks up next to us as I look over the neatly stacked piles of plexiglass. "What happened to cutting wood with the table saw?" I ask.

She shrugs. "I did one. Now I know."

I nod in understanding. That's Lily. Once is enough. She tried it and now she's ready to try something new. It's not like that with everything, but anything that doesn't catch her interest, she doesn't waste her time on.

"Alright, since you're here, will you help Sarah and me line these up?" I've memorized the plans for this geodome by now, so I just point to the various sizes. "We'll need ten of each of these on all four sides."

"Uh, Dad. This thing is round." Lily props a hand on her hip and looks at the site.

"Fine," I say, propping a hand on my hip just for fun. "We'll need ten of these, five feet from the outer base of the site, in equal piles facing the four cardinal directions."

Lily drops her hand and picks up the first triangle section. "Oh, why didn't you just say so?"

Sarah and I laugh as we follow suit. Before long, William and Charlie are bringing the base pieces over. Each step of assembling the geodome brings Sarah and me closer together. When the base is complete, Connor produces two screw guns, handing one to Sarah and the other to Charlie.

"Thanks," Sarah says, squeezing the trigger and watching the bit spin in circles.

"Lily. Mari. Will you help Grampa with the food?" I say, picking up the first frame.

Dad waves as he climbs out of his car. My girls run off, and I set the first frame in place for Sarah. "Alright, go slow until the screw gets started and then let 'er rip."

Sarah's bolder now and drives the screw in seconds. I pass her a second screw and then a third. The work moves quickly. It doesn't feel like hours as I stand inches from Sarah, holding each new section in place. William copies me, working with Charlie until we get to the last few sections at the apex of the dome. Connor steps in to drive the last few screws in place that the women can't reach.

"Do we want to stop for the day?" Sarah asks when the frame is complete.

"Are you kidding? We're almost there," Lauren says, picking up a plexiglass triangle, and I remember why I like her.

Everyone else follows her lead, even Noah. That may be the real reason they don't get along. They're both hardworking. They just never agree on how to do the work.

"That's not funny," Lauren snaps.

Noah's laughter rings out, and I remember the other reason they don't get along. I wouldn't accuse Lauren of being uptight. She might be, but I just wouldn't accuse her of it. Despite all that, she and Noah push forward when everyone else slows down, and I'm grateful. Before I know it, the geodome is assembled.

Chapter 21: Sarah

I crack open a cold beer and take a sip; my reward for finishing this project. Fortunately, there is plenty to go around and pop for the girls, because I sure didn't do this alone. Leaning on the hood of Austin's truck, I have a great view of my new greenhouse.

Noah pulls a can out of the cooler and stands next to me, crossing one foot over the other as he leans close to my side. "What'd I tell you, Sarah the Terror? Jealous as hell."

"Is that what you're doing here now, still trying to make your brother jealous?" I bounce my eyebrows playfully.

It's so strange for me to think of Austin losing his cool, but that's exactly what Noah said would happen, and he did. I feel heat creeping up my neck and pricking my ears as I remember the look on Austin's face as he chased his brother off earlier.

Chuckling, Noah elbows me. "Maybe. What about you?"

"Me?" I say, laughing, but Noah's eyes have grown serious.

"You going to keep him on the fence?" he asks. His voice is gentle, but the weight of his stare gets to me.

I'm shaking my head without knowing what I want to say. "I don't know, Noah. He is… I've only been divorced for a year. If I'm not ready, and I move too fast, what happens to Lily and Mari, let alone me and Austin?"

A heavy sigh comes from Noah, followed by a slow nod. This is a side of him I'm not used to. The looming question from the man who nicknamed me *Sarah the Terror* doesn't feel right, but I wait patiently for him to process my response.

"I guess that's fair." Noah shrugs a shoulder and takes a

long sip of his beer. Then his eyes find mine again. "On the other hand, the fact that you worry about that means you care enough about them to be good to them. Things don't always work out, but I know you're not going to tear them apart either."

He elbows me again but doesn't wait for a response. Noah pushes off the truck and makes a sharp turn to the left. That's when I notice Austin walking my way. The heat pricks again as his blue eyes study me.

"Is that man bothering you?" he asks, pointing to Noah's back, which is halfway to the front of my cottage by now.

"Always," I say with a wide grin.

Austin plants himself in the space Noah vacated, and everything about the moment feels different. As much as I enjoy being around Noah, it is nothing compared to the feeling of being this close to Austin. The heat from his body seeps through my clothes, warming my skin, and I want to curl up to him. Austin puts his arm around my shoulders, making it easier to do just that without looking like a stray cat.

Leaning into his side, I say, "Thank you."

"You're welcome," is all he says back.

We stand there for a moment as the sun dips behind the trees, filtering the light. The whole Moore clan is inside Zia Lena's cottage, and for the first time, I really think of it as mine.

My home is filled with people I care about. Even from out here, it's a good feeling.

"Dad!" Mari's voice calls.

Austin turns, removing his arm from my shoulders and taking the warmth with him. "Yeah, honey?"

"Can we have a sleepover with Aunt Charlie?" she calls back, still walking our way. Mari comes to a stop a few feet from the truck. Her smile is bright, but she is clearly tired from the day. "She said it's okay."

"Sure, honey. What time will you be home tomorrow?" Austin asks.

She shrugs. "I don't know. Sarah, you want to come too?"

"Uh, sure," I say, and for some reason, I glance at Austin,

like I need him to tell me it's okay.

His smile reassures me. "Find out what time you'll be home," he says to Mari.

"Maybe we can come over here with Sarah when Aunt Charlie goes to work."

Austin shakes his head. "Mari, you can't invite yourself to other people's houses."

"But she doesn't mind," she argues, gesturing to me. "Right, Sarah?"

I bite my lip to keep from laughing at the look on Austin's face. This is clearly a life lesson, but I really don't mind.

"Ask, first, even if it's someone as nice as Sarah," he says.

Before Austin can finish getting the words out, Mari is doing just that. "Can we come over tomorrow?"

Her eyes plead with mine, and I nod quickly.

"Yes!" Mari cheers. Then she turns to walk away.

"Sorry," Austin says, moving to put his arm around me again.

I shake my head, thinking about Noah's words. "No, don't ever apologize for being their dad. It's one of my favourite things about you."

He smiles, dipping his head slightly, like he might be blushing. I can't tell in the dim evening light, but his arm tightens around my shoulders.

"I meant sorry for her inviting herself over constantly."

"It's fine. They're great girls. I'm always happy to see them." I pause for a moment before adding, "Besides, I figure they get that from you, always coming over here, unannounced, with an army."

As I sip my beer, Austin's response is a scoff that turns into laughter. I can't hold back, and my shoulders shake as I giggle. When I catch my breath, I turn to face him.

"Thank you, really. This is above and beyond." I look at the finished geodome again. Already, my mind is filling it with dirt, plants, and a bench.

Austin's voice is soft when he says, "You're welcome," for

the second time.

I'm tempted to let Noah's advice push me over the edge. Austin's lips hover close to mine, his deep blue eyes watching me.

"Dad!" Mari calls again.

We both chuckle at the sound, but I'm the first to move. "Come on. Let's get some pizza."

Tucking his hands in his pockets, Austin follows my lead. We meet Mari halfway back to my front door.

"What's up, honey?" Austin asks.

Mari's eyes have an excited glint in them. "Aunt Charlie said we can go shopping in the morning."

"I don't know if I'm up for shopping," I say as Austin groans quietly. "How would you feel about a movie day instead?"

"Okay!" Mari turns on her heels, leading us back into the house.

"Smooth," Austin whispers in my ear. "And thank you."

I steady myself as the warmth of Austin's breath on my neck sends goosebumps across my skin. We're walking into a cottage full of people, and I'm not interested in having that discussion with any of them. Although technically, Noah and I already have. Charlie and I have, too.

Maybe I should have it with William. But I know he's stuck in his own way. *Better to get myself unstuck first.*

The chatter in the cottage is loud, with Charlie and Noah talking over everyone else. I find a spot next to Mr. Moore, who wisely took himself out of the crossfire.

"Can I get you anything, Mr. Moore?" I ask, seeing his empty plate.

He shakes his head, holding up the cup next to him. "I'm fine. Better grab yourself some before these guys clear you out. And please call me Cal."

Before I can move, Lily walks over with a plate stacked with pizza slices, way more than I can eat. "Thank you, Lily."

She smiles proudly and pulls a napkin out of her back pocket, passing it to me. As soon as she turns around, I sneak a slice of my pizza onto Cal's empty plate. He chuckles and picks it up.

"I guess since it's here," he says, taking a bite.

For a while all we can do is watch the chaos of the Moore clan, mixed with the occasional sarcastic barbs traded between Noah and Lauren. I laugh more than I can remember for a long time. Cal watches his sons proudly, laughing along with the nonsense.

"Tea?" I ask, standing.

Cal's smile reminds me of Austin when he looks up. "Sure."

A few minutes later, I'm walking back with two cups. Austin's dad reaches over to rub his shoulder, his expression pained.

"Are you okay?" I ask, feeling more than a little worried.

He waves me off before taking the cup I offer him. "Fine. Just sore. I'm not as young as I used to be."

"Are you sure?" I say, trying not to nag, but still sensing it's more.

His kind eyes wrinkle with his smile. "Now you sound like Connor. Every little ache, and he's ready to rush me to the hospital. Don't you make me feel like an old man, too."

Cal pats the seat next to him where I had been sitting. Easing into the chair, I keep an eye on him, but the pained look is gone. He sips his tea, then turns to me.

"Do you remember coming over to my house and getting stuck on the roof?"

I hide my face in one hand while I laugh. "How could I forget?"

After goading me and Charlie onto the roof, Noah took the ladder and disappeared. Zach was the one to rescue us. I knew he was really only worried about Charlie, but she refused to get down first.

"I'm glad you're back in my sons' lives," Cal says, patting my knee. "And Charlie's. They need you."

I'm floored. My cheeks twitch as I oscillate between smiling and crying. A deep breath and a long sip of tea, and I manage to say, "I think I need them too."

Cal nods, his expression is kind. Then he stands, moving to talk with Connor. My heart thrums in my chest as I process it all. The Moores have so much of my past, some of the best memories of my teenage years. I've never felt more at home than I do right now, and I can't help but think it has as much to do with this family as it does with Zia Lena's cottage.

Chapter 22: Sarah

Ida sets a bowl of peanut butter-chocolate swirl on the counter before I step all the way into her shop. The tourists crowd around, but Ida waits for me to walk up. I think this must be the day, so I pull out my wallet.

With a chuckle, Ida shakes her head. "No, ma'am."

"If you're sure," I say, acting like I'm tucking my wallet back in my bag.

As soon as Ida turns to help the next customer, I sneak a ten into the tip jar.

"I saw that," a familiar, deep voice says.

Holding my ice cream close to my chest, I turn slowly to see Cal Moore sitting at a small table at the far end of the counter. It's out of the way but close enough to the back that Ida could chat with him while she works. I suppose I should try to look contrite, but I am so happy to see Austin's dad that I just smile as I sit down across from him.

"What?" I shrug innocently.

His grin reminds me of Austin's again. "You know she gives all the tips to the kids who help in the afternoon."

"Well, then she can't get mad at me for spoiling the kids a little." It's as good a defense as I could hope for. Not that I think Ida would really mind.

Cal's eyebrows lift slightly as he nods. "I suppose that's true."

"Where's your ice cream?" I ask, taking a bite of delicious chocolate.

"Oh, I've had my allotted amount of frozen yogurt. Can't

overdo it," he says, patting his belly.

I try not to let my concern for his health show too much. Cal doesn't appreciate it, but he reads me like a book.

"I see that too. And, yes, like everyone else-" he pauses to give me a pointed look before finishing his thought. "Ida worries about me."

His smile comes out naturally, and I realize there's more to this story.

"Are you two an item?" I ask sweetly, feigning innocence.

Cal continues to see right through me. "Is that what the kids are calling it these days?" he asks with a wry grin.

"Oh, I have no idea. I'll check with Lily and Mari and get back to you."

We share a laugh, and I notice how he laughs like Noah, loud and easy. Even though he's their dad, Cal seems like he's made of bits and pieces of each of his sons.

"We haven't exactly talked about it, not in specifics."

"What?" I ask, thinking about Austin's girls. "Oh, you and Ida. Really?"

He nods, pursing his lips. "It's taken me a long time to let go of my grief. Ida is lovely, but so was my wife."

"She was very beautiful," I say, thinking of the last time I remember seeing her.

"In every possible way," he says with a sigh. "After she passed, I came here just to talk to someone who wasn't grieving as badly as I was. All of my boys missed their mom, and I didn't want to make things worse for them. Ida knew my wife, but they weren't close. So, it wasn't as hard on her to listen."

"I guess we all need that." Tears fill my eyes thinking about Sprout. I don't know why I'm suddenly so emotional.

Cal offers me a comforting pat on my hand. "For what it's worth, I'm sorry you understand grief. It's never easy. Do you want to talk about it?"

I shake my head and dab at the tear that leaks out. "Tell me more about you and Ida, please."

"Well, there's not much more to tell. After a while, I

stopped coming because I needed someone to talk to, and I kept coming because I wanted to spend more time with her. Here we are years later."

"And you've never told her how you feel?"

Cal shakes his head slowly.

"What are you two talking about?" Ida asks, walking over to us.

"You," Cal says, reaching out to take her hand.

Ida squeezes his fingers gently, her cheeks blushing ever so slightly. I stand, scraping the last bit of ice cream from my cup.

"I'd better run," I say, smiling at the pair.

"So soon?" Cal asks.

"Yeah, but I'll see you both at trivia, right?"

"Of course," Ida answers.

Before I can walk away, she's back at the counter helping another customer. As I walk out, I think about Austin's dad. I hope he works up the courage to really say how he feels. Stepping outside, I glance back to see him sitting in the same spot, watching Ida with a smile on his face.

"Trivia," I think aloud. "See you both there."

Thursday night brings us all back together at the Sandbar. The guys are already at their table when I walk in. I'm tempted to jump ship so I can sit next to Austin, but I have a plan. Walking around the table, I give William and Noah a hug first. To my amazement, Connor stands and puts an arm around my shoulders. Austin's big brother still has the warmth of a river rock, but I'm starting to see there's more going on beneath the surface.

Last but not least, I walk to Austin. He wraps his arms around me, and I lean into him as I hug his waist. "Glad you could make it," he says as he lets me go.

"Me too," I say, grinning from ear to ear.

This strange new happiness is starting to stick.

Reluctantly, I step away from Austin and find my spot at my team's table. As I sit down, Charlie appears with two plates of fries. She sets one down in front of me.

"How did you know?" I say digging in.

Charlie laughs as Austin leans over to give me a dirty look.

"Thank you," I mumble over my mouth full of fries.

Austin wraps an arm around the second plate and glares at me. Then I spot his dad walking in.

"Hey, be on my team." I say, hopping up to grab his hand.

Noah scoffs. "No fair. You can't steal Dad."

I look back at him, and he winks, a crooked grin on his face. Pulling out the chair between me and Ida, I smile sweetly at Noah. "This gives us even numbers. Makes it a fair fight."

"Sure, it does," Noah says with a big nod. "We'll see about that."

"Do I feel a bet coming on?" I ask, narrowing my eyes.

"You're on, Sarah Rossi. This is war." Noah rubs his hands together like he really means it.

I laugh as I turn back around to see Cal and Ida chatting away like they were all alone in the room. My plan is working. Satisfied, I settle in to enjoy my fries when I hear Austin clear his throat.

When I look over, his smile is something otherworldly. He gives me a small nod, and I know he approves. Suddenly, I can't think about anything else but that expression, matched with his kind, blue eyes.

Charlie returns, passing glasses of beer around the tables, and disrupting the peace as only she can. I force myself to look away from Austin and join the conversation at my table. Lauren sits down across from me, and I offer to share my fries. I hope stealing Cal does help our team, because I'm gone. My mind is lost in a fantasy.

Chapter 23: Austin

"Table three, MIT Bound and Determined, and Table four, Another Round of Pi gets it with 'Force'!" Charlie yells, needlessly loud.

"Shit, Charlie. Are you helping Sarah cheat with these questions?"

"I answered that one," Lauren retorts.

Noah rolls his eyes.

"Next question!" Charlie yells over Lauren's response. "How many seconds are in a year?"

I lean forward and snatch up a slip of paper. I scribble the answer and pass it to Noah. He glances at the response, then up at me.

"I'm not going to ask how you knew that," he says, holding the paper up for Charlie.

Lauren has their answer up too. I'm not surprised the math teacher knew this one. I won't tell Noah how I know that either. Some things a man just doesn't tell his brothers, especially not the loudmouth. Charlie darts around to all the tables to collect their answers.

"The correct answer is 31,536,000. Points for Table One, Know Moores, Table Two, Momma's Turn to Get Rowdy, Table Four, Another Round of Pi! MIT Bound, I'm disappointed in you."

Charlie lowers her chin to glower at the young guys. Two look sheepish. The third one just shrugs.

"Now, time for a break. Orders?" She glances around, pulling her ticket book out of her back pocket.

"I'm going to step outside. Be right back," Dad says to his

table. His eyes travel between Sarah's and Ida's.

I've told the guys, thank you, since last Sunday, but I want to say it to Dad again. It means a lot to me the way he's welcomed Sarah. Everyone has, but his support has always meant so much to me.

Sarah stands, and my eyes roam over her figure. I'm enjoying following her curves when I become aware of how wrong Connor is about *little Austin*. Fortunately, the memory of that comment shifts my focus. I rub my hands over my eyes. When I look up, Sarah and Ida are walking towards the washrooms.

I try not to think too hard about how good Sarah looks. *Talk about a way to complicate things fast.*

"So, did you call Bethany yet?" Noah asks.

I look around to see which of my brothers he's talking to. William shifts in his seat. "No."

"Why not?" Noah demands.

"I'm not interested."

"In women? Because her ass looked good in that swimsuit and she's a physical therapist."

"I don't think she's a physical therapist, and if you think she's so damn hot, why don't you call her?" William's voice is harsh.

"Her who?" Charlie asks, walking up with another round of beer.

Noah answers for his twin. "A woman who came into our shop and found my brother uncharacteristically charming."

William looks Charlie straight in the eyes and says, "No one."

"I am the better looking of the two of us…"

I'm consciously blocking Noah out when I hear Sarah's voice. Something doesn't sound right, and I stand.

"Are you okay?" she asks.

Then Ida joins in. "Cal, what happened?"

It's only a few yards to the far end of the bar, but I feel like jogging because of the concern in their voices.

"Dad?" I round the corner to find him limping with Sarah under one arm, trying to support his weight.

Ida is walking next to him on the other side, holding his hand. Taking in the scene, I notice his pants are torn at the knees, and he's bleeding.

"What happened, Dad?" Connor asks in his on-duty voice, startling all of us.

"Nothing. I got dizzy and I tripped."

"How dizzy?" Connor asks.

"The usual amount, I guess," Dad says, looking around at all of us.

For a moment, he seems confused, and my fear for him ticks up a notch. I step forward, and Sarah lets me switch places with her.

"I'll grab some water," she says, offering Dad a gentle smile.

"I'll get my first aid kit," Connor snaps.

It's a slow walk back to our table. I'm holding him up as he limps, wondering just how hard he fell. Finally, we get back to his seat.

Dad's still arguing. "I'm fine. This isn't necessary."

"Water is always necessary," Sarah tells him without missing a beat.

Dad concedes. "True enough. Thank you."

I watch as Sarah eases into the chair next to him. I can tell she's worried, but she continues to smile and chat. "Did you trip on the stairs?"

"No, out by my car."

"Oh, maybe some loose gravel?" she asks, taking a drink.

Dad almost seems like he's copying Sarah when he picks up the water she brought him. "Maybe."

"I'm glad you're okay. I thought you had to chase off a couple of coyotes or something."

"Oh, yeah," Dad says with a slight chuckle. "It was three coyotes and a bear."

Sarah's laugh is natural, and I can feel the tension easing in my shoulders. She brushes at the dirt on Dad's arm. "Yup, I can see the bear marks, tough guy."

By the time Connor comes back with bags of supplies, William and Noah are standing next to me. Both look as lost as I feel. Our big brother doesn't waste any time unpacking what looks like a jump box and sticking wires to Dad.

Noah scoffs. "He's awake. I don't think he needs the paddles."

"This isn't a defibrillator. It's a mobile EKG," Connor says without any humor in his voice.

"You carry an EKG machine with you everywhere?" Noah asks, leaning in to watch Connor work.

"That's the beauty of being the fire chief in a small town. I'm always on call. Dad, breathe normally and try to relax."

"That's easier said than done when you're all standing over me like I'm dead in the casket."

Instantly, William, Noah, and I take a few steps back. Sarah stands, walking over to me. She slips her hand into mine and leans on my shoulder.

"Thanks," I whisper, feeling so much more than gratitude.

Sarah nods, letting her hair tangle against my shirt sleeve. I turn to brush it down with my free hand, then pull her into a hug. With her arms around my waist, she lets me see the concern in her eyes. All I can do is nod in acknowledgement. I don't want to say anything that might upset Dad.

"Well, you're not having a heart attack," Connor says matter-of-factly, pulling the wires loose.

"I could have told you that." Dad grumbles, but the weakness in his voice doesn't match the irritation.

"But your blood pressure is too high." Connor's more forceful now. "You need to see your doctor this week, Dad."

"Okay. Okay."

They're quiet for a moment while Connor cleans the scrapes on his knees and palms. Other than being embarrassed, Dad seems like he's okay. I shudder at the thought of losing him, too. Sarah's arms tighten around me, as if she senses the fear in me.

"Dad," Connor says again, looking him in the eyes. "This week, by Wednesday."

"If you don't trust me to do it, why don't you make the appointment?" Dad grouses.

Connor stands, holding his equipment. "Done. I'll pick you up Monday morning, eight a.m."

He walks off before Dad can argue. Sarah pulls away from me and sits back down. "Hey, now that's done. Are you hungry? We could share a plate of fries."

"Sure, Sarah," Dad says. "Thank you."

"Thank *you*. I needed an excuse to get more food." Sarah stands to walk to the bar, where Charlie's taking a phone order.

With a subtle nod of her head, she motions for me to follow her. I pat Dad on the shoulder as I pass. My heart is in my throat.

"Hey," I choke when we get to the bar. "What's up?"

Sarah shrugs. "Just thought we'd let Ida have a turn to fuss over him."

I follow her gaze back to the tables. Dad and Ida are talking. She's holding his hand and motioning for him to drink the water. The scene makes me smile.

He's okay, I tell myself.

Turning my attention back to Sarah, I lean on the bar next to her. "You're pretty good at this, you know?"

"What? Eating?" She nudges me with her elbow.

Again, I feel the tension draining out of me. I elbow her back just to make contact. This close, I can smell her familiar scent of lavender. More than ever, I'm aware of how much I want to be with her, to hold her in my arms. At the same time, I know that once I do, I'll never be able to let her go.

Chapter 24: Sarah

The morning sun shines right on the picture Charlie gave me. Below the words *To plant a garden is to believe in tomorrow* sits a small begonia that Mari brought me from the hardware store. Since Lily picked out the decoration, I asked her to decide where to hang it, and the two just went together, not unlike the pair of girls who seem to spend more time here than at their house.

At first, I tried to keep Zia Lena's cottage the same. I thought it would help me feel more at home here to see it the way I remember it. As the weeks passed, I have found the Moore family has slipped into every corner of this place, and I want more of that, more of them in my life. Really, Zia Lena would have wanted it that way, too. She loved people.

A knock on the door startles me out of my thoughts, and I slosh hot tea onto the begonia.

"Sorry, Tina," I say to the plant with only three short stalks and a dozen small leaves. I'm not sure why Mari named her Tina, but that's what we call her.

I don't bother walking to my front door. I know who's there, and she always lets herself in. But the knocking continues. After depositing my cup on the small table by the couch, I move to the door. Pulling it open, I see Charlie standing there with two arms full of bags, trying to tap the front door with her foot.

"Your car is five feet from here. You couldn't make two trips?"

Charlie dashes past me, dropping the bags in a pile on the floor. "In a hurry. Have to pee."

I shake my head, laughing. You'd think I live halfway to Toronto the way she's always dancing to the washroom. While she takes care of business, I begin to unpack the bags. We volunteered to make the cupcakes for Lily and Mari's sixth grade graduation.

"Oooh, you got edible glitter. These will look amazing," I say to Charlie when she returns.

"Nothing but the best for the better-looking twins," she says with a wink.

Charlie's smile is wide, too wide. I can see red in her eyes before she turns away.

"How are you?" I ask quietly.

The heavy sigh she answers with tells me so much. I know that sigh, not just from Charlie, but from me. It's strange how Sprout's angelversary is just a few weeks before Zach's. I know most people don't think of it that way when adults pass, but everything in my world leads me back to Sprout.

"It's only been sixteen years. You'd think I'd be able to…" Her words trail off, replaced with tears.

I set down the glitter and put an arm around her shoulders. "No one ever expects you to get over losing Zach. You certainly don't have to pretend for me. Come here."

Pulling Charlie over to my kitchen table, I pull out a chair and make her sit. After getting her a glass of water and some tissue, I start the hot water for tea. Giving Charlie space is always the first step. She thinks she's stronger than the rest of us and has to bear her grief alone. I know better, but I can also keep an eye on her from the stove. After a few minutes, the kettle whistles and I pour up two cups.

"Honey?" I ask, before sitting down next to her.

"Baby," she answers weakly.

Humor may be Charlie's mask, but it's also one of the things she and Zach had in common. He loved to laugh, but the only thing he loved more than laughing was flirting with Charlie. The honey joke goes way back to when we first met the Moore brothers.

So, I keep it going with "Sugar pie."

"Honey bun." She lets out a small huff. "I miss him every day, but this time of year is the worst."

I slide the cup of tea closer, and Charlie looks up, finally. Dabbing at her bloodshot eyes, more tears glide down her cheeks.

"Don't bother," I say, shaking my head. "You're a mess. I can already see it."

"Ha! Me?" She rolls her eyes, but I can see the tension starting to fade.

We sip our tea quietly for a moment. Losing Zach to leukemia nearly broke Charlie. It nearly broke the entire Moore clan. He and Charlie married just a few short months before he passed, but there's no doubt in my mind, they were the happiest months of Zach's life.

"Thank you," Charlie whispers.

I reach over to put my hand on hers. "Can we talk about him?"

At first, she shakes her head, no. Then she gives a very slight nod. As her shoulders curl up to her ears, I try to think of my favourite memory of the youngest Moore brother.

"Do you remember when," I pause until she looks at me. "Zach convinced us he was doing a fundraiser and needed our help for a bake sale?"

Charlie barks a laugh almost instantly. "That's right.... I can't believe I forgot that."

"We stayed up all night baking and it was really all for him."

"And he hated it," she says, laughing.

"Serves him right for tricking us. He should have known I didn't know baking soda from baking powder back then." I stand and slowly make my way to the bags of ingredients.

Following me, Charlie starts to unpack everything. "If only he could see you now."

"If only." I take my time lining up everything on the counter. "Can you get me the mixing bowl?"

As we begin to work, I throw out a few more memories from our teenage summers. Charlie picks up each one, and little by little, we share the laughter and the tears of grief.

"You know he wanted a dozen children."

"I didn't know that," I say, setting the homemade icing to the side.

"He said that if he didn't make it, I should still have a dozen and name them all after him. But I just couldn't. He…"

"He was special." I finish her thought. "Here, taste this."

I hand Charlie the bowl of icing. It's a diversion to help her stay in a healthy place. The place where you feel the pain, but don't start to drown in it. Sticking her finger into the icing, she pulls out a great, big scoop. Her eyes close as she tastes Zia Lena's sweet cream cheese recipe.

"I'm so glad you got better at baking," she says, putting her finger back in the bowl for another helping.

I take a spoon out of the drawer and pass it to her. "I'll start a second batch. You look a little cozy with that one."

"I won't eat it all…" Charlie bobs her head. "Maybe."

We both laugh, then quickly look to the front door when we hear a commotion. A second later, Mari comes marching into the cottage with Lily right behind her.

"What are you two doing here?" Charlie asks, sucking on her spoon.

Mari shrugs. "Dad said we could go for a bike ride while he and Uncle Connor set up. So, we did."

"Did he know you were coming over here?" I ask.

Lily holds up her phone and then resumes tapping out a message. "Now, he does."

As Lily makes herself at home on the window seat facing the orchard, Mari comes into the kitchen. She finds a cup and fills it with water.

"Has Tina had anything to drink today?" she asks, walking away.

"Nope." I shake my head.

Charlie's head draws back, confused, and her eyebrows

knit together. "Who's Tina?"

"Our begonia," Mari says from the living room.

Nodding her head, Charlie takes her bowl to the kitchen table and sits down. After watering Tina, Mari joins her. I pass her a second spoon and lay a third on the table for Lily. She'll stay at the window for a while, I'm sure.

Quiet time, I think. It's how I recharge too. Fortunately, Charlie and Mari keep each other company. As they share the icing, I start a fresh batch. When my phone buzzes on the counter, I laugh at the text.

Austin: Please tell me my favourite twins really are with you.

Sarah: Sorry, I haven't seen Noah or William all day.

I sneak a picture of Lily curled up in her spot and send it to Austin.

Austin: Thank you. Make them ride back with you, please. I'll come pick up their bikes later.

Sarah: Sure. :)

By the time Lily joins the rest of us, Mari's face is covered in cream cheese icing.

"This is so good!" she says smiling.

Lily picks up her spoon and scrapes a delicate bite out of the bowl. When she tastes it, she pulls the bowl closer and gets a bigger scoop. "Yeah, Sarah. This is really good. What's it for?"

"It's for you," I say, surprised they don't know.

"Really?" Mari asks.

I glance at Charlie, but she just shrugs. "Yes, it's for your party today. Are you girls excited?"

"About the party or middle school?" Mari asks. "Scratch that, yes to both."

With another spoonful of icing, Lily shrugs. "I guess. I'm excited for more icing."

"Well, that's something. Do you want to help decorate the cupcakes? Aunt Charlie brought edible glitter," I say, with a smile.

"As long as I can eat more while I work," Lily says, standing.

"How about we have something with less sugar before we eat all the cupcakes?" I reach into the fridge and pull out some cold meat and cheese.

Charlie finds the bread and carries it all back to the table. As she builds sandwiches, Lily and Mari coat the kitchen and each other in sprinkles and glitter. I can't help but notice how much I'm enjoying my time with them, mess included. Wanting a family has never been a question for me. But, at this exact moment, I'm less sure of what I want that to look like. This feels good to me, like a life I could be happy with.

Chapter 25: Austin

"Thanks for your help," I say to Connor as we tie the tent onto the frame.

"Sure."

One word answers are the norm for my brother. I used to think he bottled up emotion and worried he'd explode one day. While I've seen his temper, he really just doesn't have a lot to say on most subjects. Then there are the times when he catches me totally off guard.

"You seal the deal with Sarah yet?" Connor asks, looking me dead in the eyes.

"Uh," I huff a laugh. I don't even know how to respond to that. Instead, I start unfolding chairs and spreading them out under the tent.

"Chicken," he says, following my lead.

I keep moving. "Great talk. Thanks, Connor."

I feel irritated, which is also pretty normal for time spent with my big brother. As I slam the chairs needlessly deep into the grass, Connor laughs.

"What's the deal, Austin? She's perfect. My nieces obviously love her, or they wouldn't be over there right now."

That catches my attention. I just got texts from Lily and Sarah. "How do you know where they are?"

"Because they told me where they were going before they left. Didn't they tell you?" Connor asks, picking up two more chairs and walking away.

Following him, I feel annoyed for a different reason. I like that Lily and Mari want to spend time with Sarah, but I don't understand why my girls keep shutting me out of their plans.

"They just said they were going for a bike ride. Why would they tell you and not me?" I say finally.

"Maybe because I'm not a nag."

"I do not nag my daughters," I snap, trying to think back. "Usually."

After we set out the last of the chairs, I unfold the first table. Connor picks up the end and helps me set it into place. Then we go to the next. After setting up the tables, he gives me a look.

"Are you going to answer my question?" he says, folding his arms across his chest.

Connor is only an inch taller than me, but I swear he thinks he's seven feet tall the way he tries to glare down at people by tilting his head back. I stand up straighter and stare back for a minute. Then, I cave.

"Alright, fine. The truth is, Sarah is amazing, smart, sexy..."

"Yup," Connor nods his head.

"Excuse me?"

One side of his lip lifts in a grin, and he pokes his chin out. "You heard me. Keep going."

I swallow my irritation because the truth is, I need to talk this out with somebody. "But she's only been divorced for a year, and she's dead set on having a baby. She's been saving money to see a fertility specialist."

Connor purses his lips and nods. "Here we are, back to little Austin."

"Little Austin is not a problem," I say, narrowing my eyes and pointing at him. "But what I don't know is if she'd be willing to wait to see how things go with us."

"She wants a kid, give her a kid," he says with a shrug. "Next problem."

"Really? You don't see any potential complications with that?"

"Sure, but hell, life's full of complications. Are you afraid she'll choose having a kid over being with you?"

I stop to really look in Conor's eyes. I say the next part carefully, because I need him to understand. "That's part of why she's divorced. Her ex didn't understand, and she left to start a family."

He's slower to respond this time, and I worry I've said too much. I don't want Connor looking down his nose at her. I understand why Sarah did what she did, but I'm afraid trying to explain it will make things worse.

"Well?" I say after his silence gets to me.

Connor's arms fall to his sides, and he shakes his head. "I don't think you see the way she looks at you. Whatever happened with her and her ex, there's more to it. You and I both know that. But, if you're really worried about it, stay friends."

"Just stay friends?" I ask.

"Not just friends but let her come to you when she's ready. She will, but maybe you could do a little more to show her you want more than a friendship."

"How?" I turn to walk inside, not because I don't want to hear what he has to say, but because I need to finish setting up.

Connor follows me. "For starters, you could stop acting like a nun around her."

"What are you talking about?" I pass him tablecloths and decorations.

"I've never seen you put your hands anywhere south of Sarah's shoulders."

"Damn, Connor. How closely are you watching us?" I ask with a chuckle.

Picking up stacks of plates and cups, we head back outside.

"Not that close," he says as we reach the tent. "But you keep dragging me everywhere with you, remember?"

"Not dragging you. This is your nieces' graduation. You know what? Never mind. Touch her more. That's your advice?"

"Yeah, a little affection can go a long way towards letting her know you want more from the relationship."

"I think she already knows that."

"Maybe she knows you're interested, but that doesn't mean anything. Noah's interested in half the women he meets. Then he doesn't call any of them the next day."

We spread the tablecloths over the tables, and I think about where my twins are. "Well, there's no danger of that. I have to call Sarah every other day just to find my girls. What did you get them for graduation?"

Connor laughs. "Matching pepper spray to keep the boys off them."

"Please tell me you didn't buy my daughters illegal weapons."

"No, but I wanted to. I got them both gift cards." Connor passes me half the decorations and takes the other half. "If Sarah doesn't magically fall into your arms, just talk to her. Be honest. See what she says."

Easier said than done. Nodding my head, I walk away to start hanging streamers.

I know Connor is right about showing Sarah how I feel and just laying it all out there, but he's probably also right that I'm a little bit chicken. I wonder if he's right about the way she looks at me. As much as I want to continue our conversation, William and Noah pull in, and I know that's the end of that.

When he gets out of his truck, Noah looks pissed. He's grumbling as he walks past me into my house. Then I see why. William and Lauren are stepping out of the crew cab, chatting.

"Hey guys," I say, curious about how this happened.

William nods to Lauren. "Her car's in the shop. Since Charlie is with Sarah, I offered Lauren a ride."

"Thank you, William," Lauren says, ducking her head. "I didn't realize we would all be riding together, but I, um, thank you."

She slips away quietly, and I make eye contact with William. He's grinning like a madman.

"That was underhanded," I say in a low tone.

He just chuckles. I can't help but laugh.

"How about you help me bring the food out before you

really cause some trouble."

We spend the next half hour watching Lauren both try to be helpful and snub Noah. He's more concerned about staying out of her way and sticks close to Connor, finishing the decorations. I don't know what the deal is between them, but one of these days, they're going to kill each other.

As we get closer to party time, I start to wonder if my girls are coming back. Not wanting to be a *nag*, I decide to text Sarah to see if she's on her way. I get a response, but not from Sarah, just from her phone.

Sarah: This is Lily. Mari is picking out Sarah's dress. Aunt Charlie says we'll be there in twenty minutes.

Austin: This is Dad. Why do you have Sarah's phone?

Sarah: Because she said to tell you we were coming.

I let it drop with that. Even if things don't work out between Sarah and me, I hope she and the girls stay close. They need someone like her in their lives. Jennifer would agree. My heart aches for a moment when I think of their mom missing all this. She always knew she wanted to be a mom, like Sarah.

Trying not to let myself dwell on my grief, I get busy with last-minute tasks, carrying food out, and making sure the house is neat enough for guests. The pain of losing Jennifer never fully goes away, but I want to enjoy celebrating my girls. They are growing up way too fast, and I don't want to miss it. When Sarah's car pulls up, I watch to see Lily and Mari climb out, each bringing trays of cupcakes with them.

"Hey, girls," I call, but as Sarah steps out of her car, my jaw drops.

Lily said Mari picked out her dress, and I can believe it. I would definitely not allow Mari out in public in something so form-fitting, but on Sarah, it looks amazing. The dark purple reminds me of eggplant, but the silky fabric makes it shimmer in the sun. My eyes are drawn to her tiny waist, and I have one thought.

Following Connor's advice is not going to be a problem. Keeping my hands off Sarah, that may be a challenge.

"Hey," she says softly, smoothing out the dress that doesn't quite reach her knees.

I laugh nervously, reaching for her. Sarah steps into my arms, and I savor the feeling of her so close. Everything in me wants to take her upstairs to my bedroom right now. I don't, but it's a hard-fought battle. Reluctantly, I ease myself back, taking her hands in mine.

"You, um, beautiful. You look beautiful, I mean."

Sarah's cheeks turn red. "Thank you."

Her eyes roam over me, and I'm suddenly conscious of the fact that I haven't changed for the party.

"I better go change. Do you-" I barely stop myself from inviting her to come with me. I want to. Clearing my throat, I try to suggest something else. "Would you- Wow, you look amazing, Sarah."

She laughs, and I can tell she's as nervous as I am. From out of nowhere, Charlie walks up, nudging me with her elbow on her way by.

"I should help set out the cupcakes," Sarah says, still blushing.

"Yeah, I'll be back in a few minutes."

As I watch her walk to the tent, I know she's exactly what I want. It doesn't matter to me what it takes. Babies, fertility treatments, cutting my left arm off, I don't care. All I need to know is if she wants me that way, if she wants us. Because no matter how I feel, my girls are a part of the package. But with Sarah, I already know that's not a problem.

Chapter 26: Sarah

I glance over my shoulder to see Austin still staring. I'm glad Charlie talked me into this dress. When Mari picked it out, I shook my head no before she pulled it all the way out of the closet. Charlie insisted I try it on. I'm not very comfortable showing this much skin, but the look on Austin's face was worth it. Trying not to be obvious, I watch him walk inside.

When Austin is out of sight, I focus on setting out the cupcakes without getting glitter all over me. Lily and Mari used up every ounce of the stuff Charlie bought. The cupcakes look delicious, though. As I set the last one out, I'm tempted to check my car for a sweater. It's a warm day, but I feel so exposed with the low-cut style I'm wearing.

"Hey, sexy," William says, putting an arm around my shoulders.

I laugh. "Aren't you forgetting part of that nickname?"

"I'm not picking body parts today, not in that dress," he answers with a laugh. Leaning in to whisper in my ear, he adds, "I might be jealous if I thought I stood a chance against Austin."

"Thanks," I huff.

I can always count on William to boost my confidence. He's such a good friend. I watch as his eyes follow Charlie's movement across the lawn, and I wish there was something I could do to help him.

"How's the Moore family project coming?" he asks, finally looking away and picking up a cupcake. "Have you filled your new greenhouse full of exotic flowers?"

"No, I actually ordered a couple dozen saplings to

expand the orchard. I shouldn't have spent the money, but I wanted to make sure they had time to get well established before winter."

"You could have had Austin buy them for you."

"He did order them for me," I say, a bit confused.

"Not what I meant," William says with an amused smile.

I pause to look at him, hoping for a hint, but he gives nothing away. "What do you mean?"

"I think you'll figure it out sooner rather than later." William nods to the house, and I see Austin walk out wearing a light blue button-down shirt and dress slacks. I can feel my heart jump in my chest at the sight of him.

As Austin walks straight towards me, I feel myself drawn to him, and I force myself to stand still and wait. The heat creeping up my neck makes me self-conscious, and I nervously smooth out my dress for no good reason.

"You look beautiful," Austin says again when he's close enough to say it softly to me.

I can't bring myself to answer. I feel the heat pulling at my ears, and I know I'm beet red by now. So, I nod.

"Sarah, will you help me pick out an outfit?" Lily asks.

I hadn't even noticed her walking up; my focus was so intently on Austin. She's now standing where William had been.

"Um," I hesitate, looking from her to Austin.

He shrugs, but I can tell it's not from indifference. Austin's blue eyes shine with his warm smile. I want to stay where I can enjoy the way he's watching me, but I can't turn Lily down. When I nod, she grabs my hand and drags me inside.

I planned to wrap the girls' graduation gifts this morning. When they showed up unannounced and I didn't have time, I slipped the jewelry boxes into my pockets. This dress doesn't have enough fabric for my taste, but it does have two small pockets on either side. They're more decorative, but the velvet boxes fit well enough. As my time seems to be spoken for, and wrapping them out of the question, I decide to give Lily and

Mari their gifts now. After Lily puts on the dress I picked out, I call Mari into her sister's room.

"These are for you," I say, handing each girl their necklaces. "Read it," I encourage as they open the boxes.

Mari reads aloud, "Always remember, you are braver than you believe, stronger than you seem, and smarter than you know."

Lily stares at her necklace long after Mari finishes reading. I make a mental note to spend some time with her when school starts again to help her with her dyslexia. Everything I know about Lily tells me she can do anything. I want to make sure she advocates for her needs, so nothing holds her back.

"Thanks, Sarah," Mari says, throwing her arms around my waist.

"You're welcome," I say, hugging her back.

She lets me go and turns to leave, putting her necklace on as she goes. I turn back to see Lily sitting quietly on the edge of her bed. She's holding the pendant, but her eyes have gone glassy, staring at the floor.

"What's wrong, sweetheart?" I ask, sitting down next to her.

Lily shrugs, but a sniff soon follows.

"Hey, you can tell me." I push her hair behind her ears. "Do you want me to help you put the necklace on?"

Lily passes me the pendant and turns her back to me. As I put it on, she pulls her hair to the side. When she's wearing her necklace, Lily stands and faces me.

"What is it?" I ask again.

When Lily shrugs, I reach out my arms. She steps forward and hugs me gently. It's brief before she steps back.

"Are you staying?" she asks softly.

"For the party?"

"In Osage. Aunt Charlie said you're a really good teacher and could get a job anywhere. Are you going to leave?"

"No," I say, shaking my head. If there's one thing I'm sure of, it's that I belong here. But I sense Lily's question goes deeper.

"I'm not going anywhere. I'll be here in Osage and I'll be your friend, no matter what."

"No matter what?" Lily looks me in the eyes as she asks.

"Yup." I give her a big nod, trying to make her laugh.

It cheers her up, but all I get is a slight smile. I wait a moment to see if there's anything else, but that answer seemed to be all she needed. I stand, holding out my hand to her. Lily takes it and we make our way downstairs.

When we walk outside, Lily spots some of her friends talking to Mari. She takes off across the yard, and I find myself a bit aimless. Looking over Austin's large, sunny yard, I'm impressed with the decorations. It's clear he not only loves his girls but goes out of his way to celebrate them.

"Sarah," Charlie says, walking up next to me, carrying a tray full of snacks. "Can you help Austin?"

"Sure. Where is he?"

"Kitchen." She nods towards the house, then walks away.

Making my way inside, I admire the pictures along the wall in the hallway. There's a framed photo of a woman who looks very much like Lily and Mari.

Jennifer. And I wonder what she would think of me. I am, after all, walking through her house, falling in love with her family. I hope she would like me at least.

As I walk into the kitchen, the sight of Austin causes my heart to race. For a moment, I just watch him work. Then he turns, catching me staring. His eyes light up, and I know I'm blushing again.

Without a word, Austin walks up to me, pulling me into his arms. I wrap my arms around his waist and breathe in his cologne, wishing I could fall asleep in his arms. For the first time, Austin's hands slide down my back until they land on my waist. Goosebumps creep across my skin as I lean back to look up at him.

"I'm glad you're here," he says in a voice that sounds deeper than usual.

I swallow the lump that has formed in my throat,

managing to whisper, "Me too."

All I can think about is kissing him, but he steps away. "I'd better get this food out to the kids before we have a riot."

"Let me help," I offer, remembering that's why I'm here. "What's ready to go?"

"How about you carry these bags, and I've got this," Austin picks up a tray lined with vegetables and fruit in one hand, and a bowl of dip in the other.

I laugh as I grab the bags of chips and cookies. "Do you really think the kids will eat the vegetables?"

"No," he chuckles. "But this way, Connor has something to torture Dad with later."

"How is he?" I ask, following Austin outside.

"Eh, depends on who you ask. Dad says he's fine, but Connor is pretty worried about his blood pressure."

"Oh, no. Did he get him to go to the doctor?"

Austin doesn't answer. Walking through the door, we run into Cal and Ida.

"Let me take those," Ida says, relieving me of my bags.

Cal takes the tray from Austin. "I assume this is the doctor's orders?" he asks, popping a cucumber in his mouth.

"If by doctor, you mean the fire chief, yes. Thanks, Dad." Austin turns to walk back inside.

I follow. Within a few minutes, we've cleared out the kitchen. The tables outside are overflowing with food and gifts for the girls. Finding a marker, I start handing out drinks to the kids, writing their names on the cups. Austin and I are side by side all afternoon, and I can't imagine a better way to spend a day.

As the sun sets, I'm in the same place I've spent the last few hours, next to Austin. We're moving along the tables, straightening trays, and gathering up remnants to throw away. It seems like he's stayed closer to me today, or maybe I'm imagining things.

Wishful thinking. But it doesn't feel wishful. It feels right. I need to sort out how I feel about some things. Austin deserves that much before we go any further.

With the fading sunlight, I start to shiver, and Austin steps closer. The warmth coming off him makes me want to curl against his chest. He puts a hand on the small of my back, and the shivers turn to goosebumps.

"Cold?" he asks, his breath hot on my neck.

I nod my head, turning to see his smile inches from my own.

"Be right back." Austin disappears into the house and comes back with a dark blue hoodie. Helping me into it, he zips it closed, all the way up to my chin. Then his lips twitch and his eyes narrow.

"What?" I ask, leaning closer to him.

"Nothing. Just trying to decide which I like better. The dress or the hoodie."

"Really?" I ask, cocking an eyebrow. "Can't decide?"

Austin shakes his head. "You look great either way." He rubs his hands up and down my arms. "Warm enough?"

"Yeah, thanks," I can barely whisper, feeling my heart turn flips in my chest.

As we go back to cleaning up, I catch the scent of Austin on his hoodie. Inhaling deeply, I savour the smell and feel of Austin's warmth. Even though he's standing a foot away now, I can still feel the heat from his hands against my arms.

At the end of the night, when I finally get home, I'm still wearing Austin's hoodie. He didn't ask for it back, which is good because I plan on keeping it until it doesn't smell like him anymore. Then maybe I'll trade him for another one. I change for bed, pulling his hoodie back on.

Curled up under the covers, still trying to catch Austin's scent, I think about what I want and what I really need. I think of Lily and Mari as much as Austin. My hopes haven't changed, but deep inside, I find myself letting go of my need to give birth to a child. The guilt I once felt over losing Sprout circles in my head like a faded memory. I hold onto him in my heart.

I still want the same things, but my desperate need eases

as I think about how much I love the Moores, Lily, and Mari, especially. A knot forms in my throat as I think about trying to talk this all out with Austin. I know he understands my grief, but what if we don't want the same things? What if I need something he can't provide? Then what?

Turning over, I snuggle deeper under my covers and think of Sprout again. I wish I could hold him in my arms; it's the same thing I've felt for years. But that and having another child are not the same. Maybe I'm ready to move on and accept what comes. I'm left with more questions than answers as I close my eyes and drift off to sleep.

Chapter 27: Austin

"Da-ad!" Mari sings.

"What, honey?" I ask, coming back to reality. All I can think about today is Sarah. More specifically, Sarah in that purple dress.

"Do you want us to go through this box too?" Mari asks, gesturing to the shipment of beach stuff in the middle of my store.

"Yes, please," I say, nodding for emphasis.

"Are you okay?" Lily asks, looking at me like I've lost my mind.

"Yup." *Nope.* This really shouldn't be so difficult. Sarah and I are grown adults who have both been married. We've spent more time together this summer than I did with Jennifer the first year we were dating. Of course, that was college, and Jennifer was an art major. She didn't exactly take a lot of business classes with me.

I shake my head at the tangent, letting my eyes close for a moment. *Why am I so nervous?*

The store phone rings, shaking me out of my trance. I pick up the receiver, pushing thoughts of Sarah out of my mind before I drive myself crazy. "Moore Lumber & Hardware. How can I help you?"

"Your girl just fell off her bike. I think she's hurt. Get over here," Ida says.

I know I've been struggling to stay in the moment, but I'm at least certain that Lily and Mari are still standing a few feet away, putting up stock. "Um, Ida, the girls are right here."

"Not your twins, dear. Your girl, your honey, your-- whatever you kids call it."

Sarah. "Where is she?"

"Just outside my shop."

"I'll be right there." I hang up on Ida, and call to Lily and Mari. "Stay here. I'm going across the street."

Lily turns from the Gaylord box they're working out of to nod. Mari just answers over her shoulder. "Okay, Dad."

I'm out the door before I think about telling Eric to watch the front. My girls will handle it, though. Mari knows how to keep things running, and Lily will keep her out of trouble, mostly. I don't have time to think about it as I jog across the street to where a crowd hovers around Sarah.

I can hear her talking, even though I can't see her yet. "I'm fine, really. I-"

"Excuse me," I say, pushing my way to the center.

Sarah is sitting on the pavement, holding her wrist. From the looks of things, she is not fine, but I know she doesn't want the attention, especially from a mob of mostly tourists.

I squat next to her and lift her into my arms. Her brown eyes widen, and I realize she hadn't noticed it was me.

"Sorry if I startled you. Just me," I whisper.

Relaxing against my chest, Sarah lets out a deep breath. She shakes her head. "I'm glad you're here."

I plan to set her on the bench, but as the crowd follows, I decide to carry her inside instead. A man holds open the door to Ida's shop, and I nod in gratitude as I walk in.

"Are you okay?" Ida asks, coming with an ice pack.

"Fine, I'm- ow," Sarah whimpers.

Setting her down in Dad's spot close to the counter, I look her over. Her dress is torn near the knee, and I kneel down, lifting her skirt.

"May I?" I ask, looking up at Sarah.

She huffs as she nods. I don't want to embarrass her, but I'm worried about the extent of her injuries. As I suspected, her knee is scraped and bleeding. A bruise has already started to form.

"Ida, grab us the first aid kit, please," I ask over my shoulder. Turning to Sarah, I gently lift her leg, stretching it out. "Does this hurt?"

"Not any more than it did a minute ago. I don't know what happened. I slowed down when a kid ran across the street, but I didn't brake that hard, and I just-" she stops and huffs again. "I feel like an idiot."

I nod, offering her a kind smile. "Happens to all of us, Sarah. Let me see that wrist."

Even though she only extends it a few inches, I can see what I need to. The swelling alone tells me she needs to get checked out. With Ida's first aid kit, I wrap her wrist to immobilize it. Then I clean her cuts and scrapes and give her an ice pack.

"Sarah, I want you to wait here. I'm going to get my truck and take you to the hospital."

"Okay." The fact that she doesn't put up even the slightest argument worries me. She must be in a lot of pain.

"Ida, I'm going to send the girls over. Put them to work until Connor gets here."

"Yes, sir," Ida says. "Plenty of work to be done."

I head out the door, picking up Sarah's bike on my way back across the street. I set it in the back of my truck to look at later. "Girls, Uncle Connor is going to pick you up from Ida's. Head over there as soon as you finish that box, okay?"

"What's wrong?" Lily asks. Always the intuitive one, I can depend on her to worry.

I do my best to ease her fears before they get started. "Sarah fell off her bike, but she's fine. I'm just going to take her to get checked out. We'll be back in a few hours."

"Are you sure she's okay?" Lily asks, walking closer.

I look Lily in the eyes and pause to admire her compassion. "She's fine. I promise. If you're not done with that box in thirty minutes, leave it and go help Ida, okay?"

"Sure, Dad," Mari says, grabbing another handful of

sunscreen to put on the shelf.

"Can we go over to Sarah's tomorrow to help with the trees?" Lily asks.

"We'll see." It takes considerable effort not to run out of the store, but I wait until Lily is satisfied. She needs more consideration than Mari ever does. When she nods, I'm out the door in a flash.

After Sarah limps pitifully to my truck, we ride quietly to the hospital in Barrie. I would have carried her in a heartbeat, but her chin poked up in that determined way, and I knew better than to try. Now, I'm just wishing there was more I could do. Sarah closes her eyes and leans back into the seat.

"Music," I ask softly.

She nods, and I turn on classic rock, keeping the volume low. The drive to Barrie isn't bad, and I'm relieved that Sarah's limp is less pronounced when she gets out of my truck at the drop off.

"I'll park and be right there."

When I walk inside, I find Sarah in the waiting room, holding a clipboard. She passes it to me when I sit down. "Sorry. I'm left-handed."

"I did not know that," I say, taking the clipboard and pen.

"You're about to learn a lot more." She gestures to the hospital form. "August eighth, nineteen ninety."

I jot down the answer and add her name at the top. Scanning over the familiar list of questions, I nod.

This is going to be informative, and not the way I planned on learning about Sarah.

We get through the basics without much discussion. Then I hesitate.

"Go on," Sarah encourages.

Holding the pen over the page, I ask, "List any preexisting conditions."

"None."

"Yeah, me neither."

Sarah snorts, and I look over to see her giggling. "Good to

know."

I shrug but feel better knowing this isn't freaking her out. It's the opposite. I'm reminded of how easy-going Sarah is, and why I want to know all these things. I keep reading.

"List any medications you're taking."

She shakes her head. "None."

"Really, none?"

"Nope."

"Not even--" I stop short, realizing what I'm asking. This is not the time nor the place, and I'm sure I already know the answer. A lump forms in my throat when Sarah looks up at me, curious.

"What?" Then it hits her. I can see the moment understanding fills her eyes. "Oh, um, no. I'm not taking birth control. There hasn't been anyone since Frank anyway, and with my plans it wouldn't make sense, you know?"

"Yeah, I do. I'm sorry."

She shakes her head, pursing her lips. "It's okay. I don't mind talking about it with you. I would die if I had to have this conversation with any of your brothers."

I chuckle. "Me too."

"What about you? Have you dated much since Jennifer?" I'm drawn to the tenderness in Sarah's eyes as she asks the question. I feel like we're going about this all backwards, but I guess this is as good a time as any.

Nodding, I take a deep breath. "There have been a few women since Jennifer. None have lasted very long, and it's been a few years since I've dated anyone."

Silence falls between us, and I wonder what she's thinking. I feel so comfortable talking to her, I want to tell her everything. But she shifts, and I see her wince. Wishing I could take the pain away, but knowing I can't, I try for humor.

"If it helps, I'm not on birth control either."

Sarah cracks up. "That's great. And um, anything else you want me to know?"

"No. Yes. Well, maybe when you're not all bandaged up, we

could talk more about that... um." I stare into her brown eyes for a moment, but I can't bring myself to ask her out. Not here. Not now. I point to the clipboard with the pen. "I guess we should finish talking about you first."

"Okay. If you insist."

"I mean, I can answer this all as if it were me, but the doctor may be confused when he reads your chart. You don't look like you weigh two-hundred pounds."

"You do not weigh two-hundred pounds," Sarah says, narrowing her eyes at me, but the smile is still there.

I clear my throat dramatically and hold the pen over the clipboard.

"We already answered that question. Next."

Working through the rest of the questions takes no time at all. When I finish, I turn the form into the nurse and sit down next to Sarah. She leans into my arm, resting her head on my shoulder.

"Thank you, Austin," she says, closing her eyes.

"You're welcome, Sarah. Always."

Chapter 28: Sarah

"Sarah." I hear Austin's voice, and the fog starts to clear. "Hm?"

He shakes his shoulder gently. "They're ready for you."

"Oh," I sit up, realizing that I was passed out *on* Austin. "I'm sorry."

He smiles wide. "Don't be. I ate all the snacks by myself."

"What?" I ask, looking around, still sleepy.

"I'll explain later." He nods to the nurse waiting for me.

Standing, I find my bearings and make my way across the waiting room. Things don't move much faster even after being called back. I find myself counting the minutes, thinking about Austin.

Remembering the way he picked me off the ground sends my heart racing. So much so that I'm embarrassed when the doctor comes in to talk about my wrist. Fortunately, he doesn't seem to notice.

"Looks like a mild sprain. You'll need to keep this brace on," the doctor says as he tightens the straps. "Two to four weeks, you'll be as good as new."

"Two to four weeks?" I ask, my voice sharper than I meant it to be. The trees I ordered will die by then. Not that it makes much difference. My wrist hurts so bad, I know I can't use it.

"Sorry. If you don't let it heal, a mild sprain can turn into something worse. Take Ibuprofen for the pain. Ice packs should help bring the swelling down."

"Thanks," I say sheepishly.

A few minutes later, I'm back with Austin.

"What'd they say?" he asks, standing to walk out with me.

"Mild sprain. I can't use it for two to four weeks."

"That's not too bad. Wait here. I'll go get my truck."

I nod and watch Austin walk away. My mind goes back to the two dozen saplings lined up next to my cottage. Even if I keep them watered, most of them won't make it in this summer heat. I hang my head, not paying attention when Austin pulls up.

He's holding the passenger side door open when he says, "Ready to go home?"

"Yup," I say half-heartedly. I wish I hadn't spent so much of my savings on my orchard. Things have been going so well lately that I got optimistic.

Maybe that's a good thing, I tell myself, but the self-pity lingers.

When we're waiting to pull out of the parking lot, Austin passes me a bag of M&Ms. "Saved you a snack."

"How did you get snacks?" I ask, tearing the bag open. "Since I was, um, keeping your shoulder occupied."

His smile takes my breath away when he glances over. Austin chuckles as he steers the truck out onto the highway. "Paid a kid in the waiting room to hit up the vending machine."

I laugh. "What if he was sick?"

"Nah, his big brother tripped and broke his arm. My money's on an inside job, though," Austin says with a wink. "When big brother came out, guess who signed, 'I'm sorry' on the cast."

"He didn't," I mumble over a mouth full of candy.

He nods. "See, you got off easy."

"I guess so," I say, looking at my wrist brace. *It really could have been worse.* "Thank you, by the way. For everything."

"You're welcome," Austin says, quietly. "Hey, I have an idea. There's a diner not far from here with a pharmacy right next door. We can pick up some Advil and eat."

As wonderful as that sounds, I worry about Lily and Mari. "What about the girls?"

"Oh, they're with Uncle Connor. He'll be sure they get plenty of protein and enough green leafy vegetables that they'll complain about it for a week."

"No, really?" I feel myself relaxing in Austin's company. The warm sound of his voice is as soothing as when he puts his arms around me.

"Yup. Connor's all about a balanced diet. If they get a dessert, it will be a carb… like corn."

I laugh. "He can't be that bad."

"He's a little hardcore sometimes. But don't worry. I'll feed you pancakes and ice cream if you want."

"No, I think a little protein might be good. Maybe a dessert less like corn, though."

"Deal."

By the time my head hits the pillow, I'm out like a light. Waking up, I'm remembering everything Austin did for me yesterday. I pull his hoodie tighter around my shoulders, inhaling his scent. When my mind drifts back to the conversation over the hospital form, I pull the hoodie over my eyes.

That kind of conversation couldn't have gone any better, especially given the circumstances, but I wish I'd worked up the nerve to ask him about us. I know there's time for that. It doesn't make sense to rush into anything. Even with those details out of the way, there's still a lot we need to talk about.

How can I ask about having babies before we even go on a date?

Frustrated, I push Austin out of my mind. Grasping at straws, I focus on my saplings. I need to get them in dirt as soon as possible to keep the roots from drying out. I can't dig holes, but maybe I can get buckets and fill them with dirt temporarily. Even that plan depends on a lot of heavy lifting, one-handed.

I sigh, feeling stuck. Then I hear voices. It's brief, and I think I must be losing it. Next I hear Mari's laughter. Both girls have a key to my cottage. A couple of weeks back, I had Austin make them so the girls would always have some place they could go. Their showing up unannounced is nothing new, but it is awfully early for them to be out and about.

Still in my PJs, I zip Austin's hoodie up and walk out to the living room. Lily is in her spot by the window, drawing. Mari is in the kitchen eating cereal.

"Girls, what's going on?"

Mari hops up. "Oh, good, you're awake. Now, I can turn on music?"

"Really?" I ask.

She nods. "Yeah, Dad said we can come inside as long as we didn't wake you up."

"Your dad's here?" I'm already walking towards the door.

"He's outside," Lily says.

As I walk out, I hear the faint sound of a motor running. I can't tell what it is, something small like a weed eater, maybe. I follow the buzzing out into the orchard. The morning light shining through the green leaves dapples the ground. I'm mesmerized by the simple beauty. Then I find Austin, and I'm more than mesmerized.

His back is to me as he stands with his feet wide apart, no doubt to steady him as he works. The buzzing comes from the machine he's using. It looks like a giant drill, digging up the dirt where I've marked for the new trees to go. But what captures my attention most is the way his t-shirt clings to his shoulders and back, revealing tight muscles.

I'm nearly melting as I stumble the last few feet to where he stands. I clear my throat, trying and failing to get my pulse under control. The machine shuts off, leaving only the sound of wind rustling the leaves overhead.

"Hey," he says, turning his bright blue eyes on me. "Nice hoodie. I bet it's warm."

I feel heat creeping up my neck, and I bite my lip. "It's cozy. What, um, what's this?" I point to the machine. I'm hardly concerned with the contraption. My mind is firmly fixed on how masculine Austin looks and the fact that he's here, doing this for me.

"Auger," he answers, smiling. "Makes the digging go much faster. I told the girls they had to help put the trees in and cover them, but they didn't have to help with this part if they didn't want to. They didn't wake you up, did they?"

"No," I say softly, shaking my head. "You didn't have to-"

I stop short when Austin's smile goes just a bit wider. "I know, Sarah. I want to."

Chapter 29: Sarah

Austin sent me back inside to rest. I didn't want to. Lily and Mari were hungry, so we made breakfast together, talking Austin into coming in for a short break. Having the three of them eating with me at my kitchen table felt so good. While they chat, I practice what I want to say to Austin when I finally work up the nerve to tell him how I feel. I don't come up with much by the time breakfast is over. I just know I want to be with him.

"Girls, dishes," Austin says, standing. Then he nods towards the front door. "Come with me."

I can't help smiling as all three of us follow Austin's orders. The girls go to the kitchen, and I follow him out the door. Even though Austin owns his own store, there's really nothing bossy about him. Maybe that's why it's so easy to follow his lead, because he is so kind.

We walk quietly to the center of the orchard. Then Austin stops abruptly, putting his hand on the trunk of a pear tree and turning to face me. "Look who's making a comeback."

At first, I'm confused, but then he points to the branches just over my head. I realize we're standing beneath the sick tree we pruned months ago. New growth pokes out everywhere I look.

"You saved him!" I exclaim with a slight gasp.

"*We* did," Austin corrects. "I think he'll make it after all. Now..."

He walks back to the edge of the orchard where the saplings will go in and motions to a camp chair.

"Where did this come from?" I ask.

He smiles. "The back of my truck. I knew you wouldn't sit inside on a day like this. So, I planned ahead to make you rest."

I'm laughing as I ease into the chair, being careful to keep my hurt wrist out of the way. "You really thought of everything, huh?"

"I only thought of one thing, really," Austin says in a low, gravelly voice.

The change in his tone surprises me. Then he looks me in the eyes, and I see it. Austin is looking at me like I'm the one thing. I'm who he's thinking of. I suck in a breath, ready to say what I don't even know how to say, when two voices pierce the air, breaking the moment between us.

"All done," Mari sings.

"Are we ready for trees?" Lily calls after her.

I can't help laughing. I love them, more than I ever thought possible. They're not mine, but I hope they will be. Stepmom is starting to sound as good as mom to me. Austin's smiling as he shakes his head.

"How about you go get them?" he calls to the girls.

"Okay!" comes back as a chorus, and we hear them retreat, stomping away.

"They are really excited about the orchard," Austin says, letting out a chuckle.

The warmth in his eyes is still there, but the moment has passed. If I weren't smiling so much my face hurt, I might be disappointed that I didn't finally say what I was thinking. That's when I start making my plan. I don't know how I'm going to do it yet, but I'm going to get Austin alone and talk to him, or maybe, just maybe, I'll work up the nerve to do something more to show him how I feel.

"You ready for your big date?" Charlie asks, grinning from ear to ear.

"It's not a date," I say, keeping my voice low.

"You got the kids out of the way and invited him over to your house. What the heck would you call it?"

"Keep your voice down," I say in a whisper. "I don't want the girls to hear you."

Charlie shakes her head. "I doubt they can from here with all that wind."

I glance up as if I'll be able to see the air moving around us. The evidence is everywhere. My sundress dances in the breeze while the trees behind us rustle as they sway. Checking the weather didn't occur to me when I asked Charlie to spend the day with the girls and me at the beach.

Austin and the twins stayed all day Sunday. The first thing I did after they left last night was call Charlie. I wasn't going to tell her about my plan, but when I casually suggested she and the girls have a sleepover after the beach day I invited her to, she knew what I was up to.

"I don't see what you're so nervous about. He's crazy about you," Charlie says, breaking into my thoughts.

"It's not as simple as all that," I argue. "This is just a chance for us to talk to see if maybe we want the same things."

"Mmhm," Charlie says with a dramatic nod. "Ew, that storm cloud looks serious."

I follow her gaze out across the lake to see a dark shadow moving in. As if on cue, the wind picks up, tossing the sand along the edge of the water.

"Lily! Mari!" Charlie calls to where they play in the surf. "Time to go!"

The girls splash a few more times as they come out of the water. Charlie and I begin folding up the beach chairs and packing away the snacks.

"Sarah, are you coming to the sleepover?" Lily asks.

"Not tonight, sweetie," I say.

Mari pouts. "Why not?"

"Hey," Charlie whines. "I thought this was supposed to be my sleepover, and I didn't invite her."

She gives me a wink as if that will solve anything. I laugh as Mari gives her a dirty look.

"That's not very nice, Aunt Charlie," she says with her hands on her hips.

Lily nods. "Yeah, Aunt Charlie. You should be nicer to Sarah."

"Oh, I am being very nice," Charlie grins at me. "Aren't I?"

"Yup," I say, as I look for my sunglasses.

"Please, Sarah?" Lily asks.

Turning to face her, I reach out to take her hand. "Next time. I promise. If you want, we can have a sleepover at the cottage this weekend, and we don't have to invite Aunt Charlie if you don't want to."

"She can come," Lily answers with a shrug.

"That's so generous of you girls. Let's get this stuff in my car before the wind carries us all away." Charlie begins marching to the parking lot.

She wasn't going to drive with all the tourist traffic, but I can't bike, and we decided to have a picnic at the beach. When we found a spot so close to the beach path, we should have known the weather was going to be iffy today.

"You want a ride home?" Charlie asks, looking back at the cloud over the water.

I shake my head. "Nah, I could use the walk to, um, settle."

Charlie gives me a knowing look. Settling my nerves feels next to impossible at the moment, but a walk should help.

"Bye, Sarah," Lily says, reaching to hug me.

Mari follows with another hug, and the girls climb into the car. Charlie pauses to give me another knowing, albeit obnoxious, smile.

"Call me later," she says. "Unless you're too busy to call."

"Would you stop," I say, laughing. "It's not going to be like that. We're just going to talk. That's it."

"Then I expect to hear from you later," she says, tilting

her head and bouncing her eyebrows. "If I don't…"

"Bye, Charlie!" I sing.

She laughs as she gets in her car. All I can do is shake my head as I turn in the direction of home.

As I walk, the wind continues to pick up. Lake weather can be tricky, and I'm usually better about keeping an eye on it. A sunny day can turn stormy fast, and at the moment, it feels like the storm is already here. The sky is getting darker by the minute.

I pick up the pace and start to root around in my bag for my phone. Stopping mid-stride, I realize it isn't there. I put it in the bag with the snacks, and that went into Charlie's trunk. With nothing else to do but make it home, I start moving faster. I'm trying not to panic, but I'm far enough out of town that there are no shops to take shelter in. I have no phone to call for help, and rain has started to fall.

Chapter 30: Austin

Glancing out the store windows, I see the rain coming down in sheets. Which tells me I'll have no customers and nothing to keep me occupied until I see Sarah tonight. I miss her even though it's only been a day. I miss my girls too, but I'm looking forward to being alone with Sarah at last.

The phone rings, and I snatch it off the receiver. "Moore Lumber & Hardware."

"Hey, Austin." Charlie sounds tired already. If she's smart, she'll make popcorn, put on a movie, and fall asleep on the couch.

"I guess beach day got cut short," I say, fighting a yawn.

"Yup, but the popcorn is popping. Lily and Mari are picking out a movie as we speak."

"Smart woman," I say with a chuckle. "Did you drop Sarah off?"

"No, she walked home. That's why I'm calling. Have you heard from her?"

"Sarah's out there in this?" I ask, my pulse kicking up. "Let me call you back."

I hang up the store phone and pull out my cell. It rings three times, and then I hear a woman on the other line. "Sarah?"

"It's me, Charlie. Lily found her phone in the snack bag."

"Don't worry about it. I'm heading her way now," I say, ready to run to my truck.

Charlie stops me. "Austin, let me know she's alright, okay?"

"Yup." I hit 'end' and grab my keys. "Eric, I'm going out. Have Mike lock up if I don't make it back before closing."

"Sure," Eric says from the paint aisle.

The rain is bad. I can't imagine Sarah out walking in this, in beach clothes and a wrist brace.

"What was she thinking?" I mumble.

Worse than the rain is the wind. I have to fight to keep my truck in a lane as gusts come in, pushing it one way, then the other. Wishing I had checked the weather report, I drive towards the beach, then turn down the road Sarah would have taken home. The sky looks vicious overhead. Lightning flashes, and the crack of thunder rattles my truck.

"Sarah, please be okay." My heart is pounding against my ribcage. I never used to be a worrier, but when I lost my wife, that changed. It's all I can do to steady my breathing as I scan the roadside, both anxious to find Sarah and hoping I don't find her out in this.

Driving for what feels like hours in the onslaught of rain and now debris from the wind, I start to think she must have made it home. Then, I spot a figure huddled under a tree and slam on the brakes. The truck skids momentarily, but I'm so relieved when Sarah runs up to the passenger side and jumps in.

"Thank god you're here," she says, shivering with eyes reddened from crying.

"Let's get you home," I say. I turn the heat all the way up, then pass Sarah my cell. "Call Charlie. Tell her to take the girls downstairs. I don't like the look of this."

Straightening out the wheels, I ease my way through a puddle that nearly covers the road. The wind continues to batter my truck. Nothing about this feels safe, but if I drive any faster, I'm likely to end up skidding off the road.

"Hey Charlie, it's me," Sarah says. Her voice is shaky as she continues to shiver. "No, I'm fine. I'm with Austin. We're driving to my cottage. He said to take the girls downstairs. Keep your phone on, in case there's a weather alert. Okay. Bye."

She passes my phone back and wraps her arms around

her body, trying to fight off the cold.

"We're almost home, Sarah." I want to reach for her to hold her hand, but I can't right now. Keeping the truck on the road is all I can manage. Finally, we turn down her driveway, but my relief is short lived. A tree has fallen. A huge log blocks our path, and there's no way I can get around it on either side.

I look over at Sarah. Her eyes are staring at the tree like it's a mirage that will evaporate. Putting the truck in park, I cut it off.

"We'll have to make a run for it," I say.

She nods mechanically, still shaking from head to toe. I open my mouth to reassure her, but then my phone goes off. It's not ringing, it's squawking. Sarah's eyes meet mine. We both know what that means, but I look anyway. *Tornado alert.*

"We've got to get inside." I don't wait for her to answer.

Throwing my door open, I leave the keys in the ignition. Sarah is reaching with her good hand, trying to find a place to hold on to as she gets out. I run around to help her down. As I round my truck I see the clouds beginning to churn into a funnel.

We rush to climb across the fallen tree, but Sarah's legs can barely straddle the trunk. I pick her up and set her on the other side of the log.

"Run, Sarah," I shout, but she reaches for my hand, waiting for me.

Grabbing her hand, we sprint to her front door. I catch Sarah more than once as she slips in the mud.

Once this is over, I'm ordering more gravel for this driveway. There's no time to laugh at the thought, though, the noise from the storm picks up as we run. I know it's heading our way, as if the tornado is chasing us into Sarah's cottage.

She's fumbling with the keys when I look back to see the funnel cloud touching down. The keys hit her front stoop with a smack, and I snatch them up.

"I've got it," I say more to myself than her.

Sarah looks back, and I know she sees the funnel, because

her eyes come back to mine filled with fear.

"We'll be fine," I say calmly as I get the key in the lock and push open the door.

Slamming the door shut against the wind, I lock it for no good reason. It's the windows we have to worry about, and Sarah doesn't have a basement. I grab her hand, pulling her towards the center of the house. As we pass by the couch, I take the blanket hanging over the back and wrap it around Sarah's shoulders. She is soaked from head to toe.

The kitchen is the closest thing we have to shelter, but as we reach it, Sarah stops and darts back the other way. The blanket falls to the floor.

"Where are you going?" I shout.

"Tina!" Sarah yells back. "She's too close to the window!"

"Who in the hell is Tina?"

Sarah comes running back with a potted plant. "She's Mari's begonia."

I'm touched and horrified that she's worried about a flower at a moment like this, even if it is Mari's flower. I have hundreds of begonias at my store, in dozens of colours. Mari can have all of them for all I care. Taking the pot from her, I stuff it in the fridge and slam the door.

"There, Tina's safe. I need you to be too."

I'm wrapping the blanket around Sarah again when the windows start to crack. Then they're shattering as the wind throws limbs through them. From the window where the begonia sat, a branch crashes in, carried too close to where we are by the fierce wind.

"Get down!" I push Sarah to the floor and crouch over her, wrapping her in my arms. "Pantry," I say.

Sarah starts scooting backward. I follow on my knees. As we move closer to the pantry, I keep her shielded as best I can. I tower over her, but we seem so exposed, even on the opposite side of the counter from all the windows, or where the windows were.

She folds up, tucking her knees close to her chest when

we reach the corner. Wrapping one arm around her legs and the other over her head, I nearly cover her from head to toe. Sarah is still shaking, and I reach up to pull the blanket tighter around her shoulders.

"I'm okay," she says in a low voice, barely audible over the sound of the wind and rain.

Her breath is warm against my damp skin, and I feel a tingle that drowns out the storm raging around us.

"Me too," I rasp, feeling so many things at once. My heart pounds in my chest, and all I can think about is the woman in my arms. A crashing sound makes Sarah jump, and I snuggle her closer.

"I've got you," I say, and her muscles relax, trusting me in a way I never knew I needed until this moment. A lump forms in my throat, and I close my eyes, waiting for the storm to pass.

Chapter 31: Sarah

The sound of the wind is deafening as the tornado seems to sit on Zia Lena's cottage. Thunder breaks up the howling from time to time, rattling everything that isn't already broken. I can't tell anymore if the house is shaking from the storm, or if it's just me trembling from how cold I am.

Walking home did my nerves no favours. I was quickly soaked from head to toe when the rain started. Then I noticed the headlights coming. I ran off the road to avoid getting hit. It never occurred to me that Austin had come looking for me. I cried when I recognized the logo. Running to his truck, my mind thought of leaping into his arms, but the storm was already raging. Little did I know that was just the beginning.

Despite the fact that it sounds like my house is coming down around us, I am keenly aware of Austin's breath. He's holding me so close, I can practically hear his heart pounding in his chest, and feel his warm breath on my neck as he protects me. My pulse is racing to the point I can hardly breathe, but I feel so safe, tucked in Austin's arms, his body shielding me from the storm.

"I've got you," he whispers again. At least it sounds like a whisper, fighting to be heard over the hail pounding the cottage.

I lift my head to respond and find that I'm tucked under his chin, my lips only able to reach his neck. If we weren't sheltering from a tornado, I'd kiss him there. Suddenly, my heart is pounding even harder as thoughts of being with Austin fill my mind. The storm becomes background noise as I imagine our life together, never having to wonder if he's there for me, if he's going to take care of me.

Over the course of this summer, Austin has shown me he's got me in so many ways without even having a reason for it. He's never pressured me to do anything, other than get on that skid steer. I find myself smiling into his neck, knowing I'd probably look crazy if he could see my face. But it's hitting me now how much I love him, truly love the man that he is. We haven't even kissed, and he has loved me better over the last few months than anyone ever has.

The sound of another tree coming down startles me out of my thoughts, and I flinch. Austin pulls me closer to his chest, reassuring me that we are safe. More importantly, we are in this together.

A crackling sound is followed by a loud thud, and we know the tree has broken apart somewhere close by. I'm huffing, trying to catch my breath, but at last the sound of the wind and rain starts to ebb, ever so slightly.

"We're almost there, Sarah," Austin says.

I nod, pressing my forehead into his neck, needing to be as close to him as I can, just waiting for this storm to pass. Minutes tick by, and I notice the sound of my breathing. Little by little, Austin begins to pull back as we hear the fading sounds of the rain moving away. Bits of debris caught up in the storm continue to shower down. We can hear it drop against the roof, like the tingling of ice in winter. The sounds continue to fade until it's just us.

Austin sits back, and I wonder how long he was crouched over me. He groans as he shifts, leaning against the cabinet and stretching his legs out. His blue eyes are tired, but they are fixed on mine.

"Are you okay?" he asks, his chest heaving with deep puffs of air.

Nodding, I swallow the lump in my throat. I don't even know what to say after all this. The storm has left my house in tatters, but I can really only think of one thing--how Austin risked his life for me.

He holds out his hand. I place my hand in his, and he tugs me gently. I'm not sure if he feels exactly the way I do, but I can't wait any more to find out. Words fail me, so I act, climbing into his lap and pressing my lips to his.

At first, Austin is still, and I worry I've done the wrong thing. Then he lets go of my hand and wraps his arm around my waist, pulling me closer. He shifts his legs, so my knees fall to the side, straddling him. Cupping my face with his other hand, Austin's mouth presses into mine, making me feel desperate for a taste. I lick his lips, and he follows suit, deepening the kiss.

Lost in his kiss, I wrap my arms around his neck, his hand slips from my face and wraps around my back, pulling me against him with both arms. Austin's strength has me melting into his embrace. My heart races, but I don't want it to stop. I want this. I want him.

His fingers thread into my hair, pulling my head back and his kisses move to my neck. I can't think or breathe, and I don't want to.

"Sarah, I-" Austin stops, his lips pressed into the soft part of my shoulder at the base of my neck. His breathing is heavy, but he slows, easing me back as I rest in his arms. Even though I don't want him to stop, I'm met with a brilliant smile that tells me everything is okay.

Austin's blue eyes sparkle as they dance over me, taking in every inch of what I'm sure is a messy version of what I want to look like. He chuckles and pulls me close again. I want more kisses, but he brings my head next to his and holds me tenderly.

Time slips away again. I have no idea how long he's held me, but I don't ever want it to end.

"You're all wet," he mumbles in my ear, making me laugh. "And now I'm all wet."

I'm giggling when I say, "I have a hoodie you can borrow."

"Sarah, I-" he starts again, letting me sit back, still in his lap, still in his arms. But I can see his smile again, and I'm grateful for it. "What did you want to talk to me about?"

I'm laughing now. What can I possibly say? "Um, I was just

thinking maybe you and I, if you're interested, I mean, we could um…"

Austin's smile disappears as he pulls me into another time-halting kiss. His lips move over mine, kissing the edges of my mouth, before coming back to the middle, tasting me all over again.

"I guess that'd be okay," he says with his lips still touching mine, ignoring the fact that I didn't even finish the question.

But it's not really a question anymore. I know how I feel about him, and I know how he feels about me. Maybe there are a few more things to discuss, but there will be time for that. We've got all the time in the world.

Chapter 32: Austin

Pressing my lips to Sarah's, I squeeze her tighter. Kissing her is better than I imagined it would be. I want to stay here, tasting every inch of her skin, or better yet, take her to her room. I could get lost in her softness, but as I stroke her back, I feel her clothes still damp and her shivering.

"Hey," I say, trying to pull away from her lips. Instead, I land on her cheek, kissing her again.

Sarah's eyes are closed, and a smile plays on her lips. "Yeah," she answers, her voice a huff of hot air on my face.

Applying every ounce of self-control I have, I loosen my hold of her. Sarah is so relaxed in my embrace, she eases back into my hands. As I steady myself, her brown eyes watch me. Getting caught up in her beauty, I pull her closer, kissing her gently one more time. She shivers again, and I know she needs to get out of those wet clothes.

"Um," I try again. This time, I hold her tight as I say what I was supposed to say the first time. "You want to put on something warmer?"

"Oh," she sighs, leaning her forehead against mine. "I probably should."

"Before you go, Sarah," I ease her back again so I can look her in the eyes. "I'm glad this happened. Not the storm, but us. I know there's more to say, but this isn't a momentary thing for me."

Her smile goes wide, and a lovely shade of red colours her cheeks. Then she dips her head, and her eyes close. For some inexplicable reason, a moment of nervousness grips me.

"Sarah?"

She looks up, grinning from ear to ear. "I'm really happy to hear you say that."

Relief rushes through me. I know I shouldn't be so insecure, but the stakes with Sarah are high. We haven't even talked about our future, and I'm scared of losing my chance.

"Let me help you up," I say, lifting her at her tiny waist.

Sarah's wobbly as she stands. Between sheltering from the storm and shivering from the cold, it's been a tough few hours. When she's standing, she offers me her hand.

It takes Sarah and pushing off the cabinet to get off the floor. "Thanks."

This is the point I should let her go change, but I pull her into my arms. Sarah comes easily, wrapping her arms around my waist. My phone rings in my pocket. So, she steps back as I pull it out.

"It's Charlie," I say, accepting the call. "Are you and the girls okay?"

Sarah's eyes are full of concern as I talk to my twins, and it reminds me of why I love her.

"Are they okay?" she whispers.

I'm nodding as Lily asks about Sarah. "Yes, she's fine, sweetheart. No, she's standing right here. Hold on."

Turning on the speaker phone, I hold it out to Sarah. "Girls, are you okay?"

"Yes, that was scary," Lily says.

"So scary," Sarah says. "It broke all my windows."

"No way," Mari answers. "Is Tina okay?"

"Yes," I grumble. "Tina is fine."

I don't mean to sound annoyed, but Sarah could've gotten hurt going after that plant, but the relief in Mari's voice tugs at my heart.

"Sarah made sure she was safe," I add, smiling at the woman in front of me.

"Thank you, Sarah!" Mari sings.

"Alright, girls. Sarah and I need to go. Let me talk to Aunt

Charlie for a minute."

There's a good bit of commotion before I hear Charlie's voice. "Hey, Austin. Are you really okay? The news said it hit that area head on."

"We're fine. Sarah's cottage will need repairs, but we're good," I'm looking into Sarah's brown eyes as I say it, and it means so much more than surviving the storm. "How is your house?"

"Fine. I'm sure there are a few loose shingles and whatever, but nothing major."

"Okay, good." I think about telling Charlie that I'll bring Sarah by later, but I don't. That's probably what will happen, but at the moment, I'm entertaining the idea of taking her home with me. "I'll check in with you later. Make sure the girls charge their phones."

"Yup, I'm on it," Charlie answers.

I hit "end" and tuck my phone back in my pocket. "You should probably pack a bag," I tell Sarah.

Her eyes widen as if it's just hitting her that her house has been damaged pretty badly. I gently rub her arms, "Don't worry, Sarah. We'll get it put back together in no time."

"We?" she asks, looking up at me as if the question is so much more than the house. Her hands rest on my chest, and her faith in me is evident by the look in her eyes.

Taking a deep breath, I put it all on the line. "Yes, Sarah. I'm in love with you. If you'll let me, I'll do---" I stop short, trying to sort out what needs to be said, what needs to wait, and my mind is reeling from the onslaught of thoughts.

"I love you, too," she says before I can get myself together.

Her words hit like a hammer, but instead of hurting, they solidify things for me, telling me the only thing I need to know. Everything else is covered, or at least we'll figure it out together. "I love you, Sarah."

While Sarah changes, I take a slow walk around her living room, surveying the damage. The windows are all blown out, but the trees seem to have missed the cottage. I'm about to walk outside when I hear Sarah calling for me.

"Yeah," I answer, walking into her bedroom for the first time. It might be romantic if not for the broken glass and the breeze coming through the window with a branch sticking through it.

Sarah is standing by her dresser holding an overnight bag. Her eyes are tired, and she's clearly overwhelmed. "How long do you think it will be before I can come home?"

"Few days, I guess. We can get heavy duty plastic to cover the windows temporarily. I've got the number for a storm recovery crew."

"Is that expensive?" she asks, scanning the room.

I step forward and take her free hand in mine. Not wanting to add to her overwhelmed emotions, I chose my words carefully. "If you'll let me, I'll take care of that. Is that okay with you?"

Her eyes search mine for a moment before she nods. "Thank you."

"You're welcome." I offer her a smile, feeling pride that she's willing to let me take care of things for her, and hope that this is just the beginning. "Do you want me to stay here with you while you pack? I was going to check on things outside--"

"Stay," she answers, smiling weakly.

"Sure." I reach for the bag in her other hand. "I'll hold this. You can stuff it full."

Sarah laughs. "Or you could set it on the bed. I'm not totally helpless, even in this brace." She holds up her arm and makes a funny face.

"Fine, but make sure you pack that dress you wore to the girls' graduation."

"You're going to be a lot of help, aren't you?" she says, putting a hand on her hip.

I shrug, trying to look innocent. "Depends on what you mean by help."

Rolling her eyes, she turns to open a drawer. I'm tempted to study the contents, but I'm getting ahead of myself. Instead, I keep her talking about nothing, chitchat to keep our minds off the storm.

In no time, Sarah is zipping up the bag and pulling my hoodie around her shoulders.

"I guess you're coming home with me," I say, tugging on her sleeve.

"I am?"

I pick up her bag off the bed. "Well, yeah. That's the only way I'm getting my hoodie back."

Sarah giggles. "You're never getting this back."

I chuckle as I follow her out of her bedroom. Sarah stops by the fridge and pulls the begonia out.

"Tina's coming with us," she says, walking out of the kitchen.

When we get to her living room, Sarah sucks in a breath. Water puddles around broken glass in nearly every corner. I put my arm around her shoulder. "We'll get this cleaned up. Don't worry."

She nods slowly and walks towards the door. Opening it, she pauses to look around one more time. "I don't know what I would have done if you weren't here."

"You would have been fine," I say, somewhat convincingly. Truth be told, I don't even want to think of Sarah going through this alone.

"Can we check on the greenhouse?"

"Of course."

The geodome survived the tornado without any real damage. It doesn't look pristine anymore, but we secured it to the foundation well. After we look it over, we check on the raised beds. A lot of the vegetables were damaged, but many are fine. Sarah takes it all in stride.

When we're finally ready to leave, it's a long walk back to

my truck, and we take it slow. Fortunately, it survived the storm relatively unscathed. The bed is full of smaller limbs and debris, but the windshield and windows are still there. A crack runs down the passenger side, but I can't tell what made it. It's still safe to drive, though. The windshield is just something else to be taken care of after a good night's rest.

"Should I drop you off at Charlie's?" I ask as I back out onto the road. I don't want to, but I don't want to push Sarah either.

Before I can overthink it, she shakes her head. "Would you mind if I stayed with you?"

"No, I don't mind." Feeling a fresh wave of joy, I drive towards home.

Chapter 33: Sarah

I should be nervous walking into Austin's home after asking to spend the night with him, but I'm not. The storm may have something to do with that. I'm so tired at this point, I could have slept in my own bed with the wind blowing in from outside. But there's also the way Austin makes me feel safe whenever we're together. That's what I need right now.

Seeing my living room in pieces shook me more than I wanted to let on. I really don't know what I would have done if Austin hadn't found me. I'm not sure I would have made it home at all. A shiver runs down my spine at the thought.

Austin sees right through me. He sets my bag down behind his couch and pulls me into his strong arms. "We're okay. I've got you."

And I believe him. Rather than answering, I simply lay my head on his chest. After a moment, I let him go. My arm is getting tired, and I'm still holding Tina.

"Let me take that," Austin says. He sets the plant on a small table near a window. "I'm going to walk around the outside of the house, just to make sure there's not any damage. Make yourself at home, okay?"

"Yup," I say with a nod, but when he comes back, I'm still standing there.

I'm in the same place Austin left me twenty minutes ago. I feel like a statue, unable to move. Grabbing my bag and taking my hand, Austin leads me upstairs to his bedroom.

"The washroom is through there," he says, pointing to a door on the far side of his room. "Why don't you freshen up, and

I'll get you some fresh sheets."

"You don't have to do that," I say.

"If my mom were alive today, she would say otherwise." Austin's smile distracts me as he winks. Then he's turning to leave.

After he's out of sight, I dig in my bag for my PJs and toothbrush. While I change, I admire how clean his washroom is. Mine is rarely this clean. I'm not messy, but I hate scrubbing grout tile.

Will Austin be okay with that?

My heart skips a beat with the thought of us together. We haven't been on a date yet, and I'm already worried about how clean my shower is. Taking a deep breath, I remind myself that I just survived a tornado. It's not the time to overanalyze things.

With Austin's hoodie on over my PJs, I walk back into his room. He tucks the last corner of a fitted sheet onto his bed and looks over, grinning.

"I have other hoodies."

I laugh. "Then you should be fine without this one."

Taking a few steps towards me, Austin looks every bit as mischievous as Noah when he says, "What if I want that one?"

"Are you going to fight me for it?" I ask, expecting him to pick at me the way his brother would.

But Austin's eyes grow soft as he looks me over. He shakes his head slowly, pursing his lips. "Nope."

He kisses my cheek, then takes a step back. Picking up a flat sheet, Austin finishes making the bed while I watch. He lays out a quilt, then looks up at me with those beautiful blue eyes.

"I'll be on the couch, if you need anything."

I shake my head.

Austin nods as if he understands. "Okay, see you in the morning."

"No," I manage to say.

He waits for more, but I don't know how to ask a man to stay in bed with me. I know it's too soon for intimacy. That's not really what I want. I want that with Austin, but at the moment, all I really want is for him to make me feel safe the way he always does.

But this is his bed. If I ask him to stay, is he going to expect something different? He knows I'm not on birth control. At that thought, I feel heat flood my features. I know I'm blushing beet red. I put a hand over my eyes.

"I'm sorry," I mumble, not looking at him.

Austin's arms are around me a moment later. He presses a gentle kiss to my forehead. "No need to be sorry. How about I keep you company until you fall asleep?"

"Would you mind?" I ask, my face still hidden.

"Not even a little bit," he answers, kissing me again. "Do you mind if I put on my PJs?"

"No," I squeak out. I know I'm being ridiculous, but Austin is being so understanding, I'm enjoying my own goofiness.

I hear him moving around, opening and closing his dresser, and then the washroom door closing. Rather than continue to fixate on my nerves, I decide to climb into bed.

Austin's bed.

But as I lay down, it's not awkward at all. The clean sheets feel nice, and I immediately start to drift. My eyes pop open when I hear Austin coming out of the washroom, and I know I have fallen asleep. I still want him here with me, though.

I pull back the covers and wait for him. The t-shirt and boxers he wears allow me to see plenty of muscle, and my heart flutters, causing me to second-guess what I want from tonight.

"Sarah, can I ask you something?" Austin says, his voice deep. He turns off the lamp and slides under the covers, facing me. "Since we're alone in bed together."

I swallow the lump that quickly forms in my throat and nod. "Sure."

"Will you be my girlfriend?"

My eyes shut as I let out a peal of laughter. Still giggling, I open my eyes and Austin's smiling back at me in the dim moonlight.

"What do you say, Rossi? Can we make it official?"

"Yes, Austin. I will be your girlfriend. Will you be my boyfriend?"

"Depends, do I get my hoodie back?"

"Nope, as boyfriend and girlfriend, possession of the hoodie and all other sweatshirts passes to me, the girlfriend."

Austin laughs a deep belly laugh. "I guess I can live with that. What about the dress?"

"The dress?" I ask, confused.

His eyebrows bounce once as that mischievous Moore grin spreads across his face. "The purple dress?"

I shake my head, trying not to laugh. "I don't think it will fit you."

"No, but I know someone it does fit, and as her boyfriend, I reserve the right to ask respectfully that you wear it next Saturday."

"What's next Saturday?"

"Our first date."

I can't explain the joy I feel at this moment, but I see it on Austin's face, reflecting at me. It feels big, heavy, as if we both know this is the start of something wonderful. But I can't be serious with him, or maybe it's because of all this, that I know I don't have to be.

I pretend to be serious when I ask, "Our first date? You mean this doesn't count?"

"Can't," Austin says, straightening his lips into a scowl. "You think I'd let a girl come home with me on a first date. You're crazy."

Then there's a staring contest to see who can keep a straight face the longest. Austin wins by a hair. As soon as I smile, he laughs.

"Besides, what kind of example would that set for my girls?" Austin asks the question while still laughing, but it catches my attention.

"What do you think they'll say?"

His smile is breathtaking as he studies me. He reaches over, placing his hand on mine. "Sarah, they adore you. And I know you love them. That's part of why I fell in love There are so many reasons, but the way you accepted them, your life, did so much for me."

"I do love them," I say, softly. "You're doing an amazing job raising those girls."

"They're my whole world," Austin says easily.

Then he squeezes my hand, drawing closer to me, head to toe. There's still enough space between us that he's looking me in the eyes, but I feel his warmth, and I'm drawn to it. His thumb rubs circles on my wrist as he speaks.

"Sarah, I know this is all new, but I want you to know that my world can get a little bigger. What I mean is, I hope you'll give me a chance, give us a chance. I know you want to have children of your own, but I'm hoping that can be something we do together."

I'm stunned, left completely speechless. It's the one thing I thought I'd have to give up having a life with Austin. To hear him say that, to offer that, breaks my heart in the best way.

"I'm sorry," he rasps.

And I can only assume my silence gave him the wrong impression. I stop him with a kiss. It's nothing like the searing heat from earlier today, but it's tender and sweet, like he is.

"Thank you," I say, pulling back to look into those blue eyes. "I want that for us. I want *us*."

I see Austin's warm smile for a moment before he pulls me into his arms. I'm so tired and so happy that I close my eyes. The next thing I know, it's morning.

Chapter 34: Austin

The sun shines in my eyes, making me blink as I yawn. At first, I'm not quite in touch with my surroundings until the woman in my arms stirs.

"Good morning," Sarah whispers into my chest.

Pulling her as close as I can, I kiss the top of her head. "Good morning."

I could stay like this all day. No part of me wants to let Sarah out of my bed, but I know that it's coming. Even though all we did was sleep, the talk we had last night made me feel like we are on the same page when it comes to our future. At least the long-term. I have a feeling I won't be able to convince Sarah to stay with me again tonight.

"Um, I need to get up," she says without moving.

Loosening my grip, I lean back enough to see her smiling up at me. "Okay."

Sarah doesn't move.

"I thought you needed to get up."

"I do, but you're so warm. I don't want to."

I laugh, running my fingers up and down her arm. "Stay as long as you want."

"But, I have to pee."

"Well, then you'd better scoot, but I'll still be here when you get back."

Sarah wiggles to the edge of the bed. "Promise?"

"I'll keep your spot warm," I say with a smile.

At some point in the night, Sarah must have gotten too warm. My hoodie is gone, allowing me to admire her figure as she walks away. I suck in a deep breath to steady myself. I'm rushing things. I know I am, but I can't help it. I'm in love with her. She's beautiful, and I know she loves my girls like they're her own.

What more could I ask for?

When Sarah comes out of the washroom, I'm struck again by her beauty. Her tousled hair hangs over her shoulders, drawing my attention to her figure. I have to look away for the sake of my self control. As she climbs back into my bed, I close my eyes and take a few deep breaths.

"What are you thinking about?" Sarah asks as she snuggles against my chest.

I'm thinking that may be a trick question as my fingers glide up and down her arm.

"You," I say with a sigh. Forcing myself to think about anything else, I change subjects. "And the girls. Charlie has to work today, so I need to pick them up in a few hours."

"I guess you should drop me off at her place."

"I should?" I ask, holding back the groan dying to get out.

"Well, we do want to set a good example for the girls, right?"

"I guess I have to agree to that. For the record, I don't want to."

"But this is going to seem new to them, and I don't want them to get the wrong idea."

"Yeah," I answer, begrudgingly. "But that doesn't mean I want you to go." To prove it, I lower myself to Sarah's lips. Indulging in a few deep kisses pushes me to my limit and I pull back. "Before I let you go, can I just say how happy this makes me."

"What?" she asks, smiling.

"This," I say, kissing her soft lips again. "I love you."

"I love you, Austin."

For a long time, I hold Sarah, listening to her breathing softly. The sunshine tells me it's mid-morning, and we need to get moving. Everything in me wants to savor this moment between us. So, I do. Charlie will call me or just show up if she needs to. I doubt Sarah would feel comfortable getting caught in my bed at this point, but I'm willing to risk it. It's been a long time since I've felt this way, and if losing my wife taught me one thing, it's that I can't take one single moment for granted.

When nature calls, and I have to get up, I kiss Sarah again. "Stay here as long as you want. I'm going to start some coffee and get dressed."

"Okay," she whispers, pulling the covers up around her shoulders.

I take care of business, stop to kiss Sarah again, then go downstairs to the kitchen. Once the coffee is brewing, I head back up to get dressed. All I can think about is how I want this to be my life, to have Sarah here with me when I go to sleep and wake up in the morning. I remind myself not to rush things as I grab a change of clothes.

"I'll use the girls' washroom," I tell her. "But take your time."

"No, I'm ready," she says, sitting up.

Me too, I think to myself. *Me too.*

It's been just shy of a week since the tornado, but Sarah was able to go back to her cottage yesterday. That's where I'm picking her up for our date. Before I knock on her door, I check the pallets of building supplies I had delivered. Right now, her windows are covered in heavy-duty plastic, but next week I'll be over here with Connor to install the new ones. There's just one minor detail I need to discuss with her before we get started.

I knock on her front door, feeling as giddy as a teenager. When Sarah comes to the door, I reach for her, pulling her into a kiss.

"Hi," she says, smiling up at me a moment later.

"Hi," I answer with my hands on her waist. "Are you ready for our first official date?"

"Maybe. Is this okay?" She holds her arms out, and I lean back to look at her dress.

I wanted her to wear the purple one, but it would have been too cold for my plans tonight. So, I called her this morning and suggested something comfortable and warm. Sarah has on one of her long flowing skirts and a top that's too loose for me to admire her figure from a distance. Fortunately, I don't have to keep my distance.

"You look beautiful," I say.

Her cheeks turn red, but she doesn't hide her face from me. Sarah's smile, blushing or not, is one of my favourite sights. I take her hand in mine and walk her to my truck. The weather turned out perfect tonight, and I'm excited to see what Sarah thinks of our date. In the corner of my mind, I worry that she won't like what I have planned for the cottage. But I remind myself that I already know we want the same things. The supplies I ordered are just part of making those dreams a reality.

After parking by the beach, Sarah and I meander slowly towards the surprise. My brother has the campfire burning nicely, and I can see it from here. We chat about our week, until Sarah spots William. He waves before walking back to his car.

"You planned all this for me?" Sarah asks when we reach the picnic.

"Don't sound so surprised," I say, opening the basket and pulling out the wine glasses.

She laughs. "I am a little surprised."

"Why?" I open the bottle and pour us both a glass of what Charlie claims is Sarah's favourite wine.

"Just that you would go so far out of your way for--" she shrugs her shoulders, taking a sip of the Merlot.

I shake my head. *How do I get her to understand?*

"Sarah, you know all the building supplies I had delivered to the cottage?" It's a strange segway, but it's the only way I know to help her see where I'm going. Although I kind of hoped she already did.

"Yes, that looks expensive. I hope you didn't go

overboard."

"I don't care about the cost. What I care about is the door underneath all those windows."

"The door?"

Now I have her attention. "Yes. There is a door that I plan to install on the back side of the cottage, where a window used to be. Where Tina's window was, actually."

"Okay? I already have a back door, though."

"You do, but I plan to keep that one as a back door. The other one is temporary. It will make it easier to add onto the cottage." I pause to let her absorb that detail, taking a long sip of wine. It's not my favourite, but none of this is really about me.

"What are we building on?"

"An extra room for the girls and a nursery."

Sarah's jaw falls open, and she nearly drops the glass of wine. She's stammering when I reach over to take her glass. I set the wine aside and take her hands in mine.

"I want to make you the happiest woman in the world, Sarah. I want to give you as many babies as you want and a beautiful home to raise them in. I can't think of a more wonderful place to raise our children than in the cottage that you love."

Tears fill her's eyes until one slips out. I reach up and brush it away.

"If you'll let me try, Sarah, and if we can't have children on our own, I'll do whatever it takes, fertility treatments, I don't care. All I want is us, our family, you, me, the girls, and however many little ones we've yet to meet."

Sarah tilts her head back, letting the tears run down her cheeks. "Okay."

"Okay?" I ask, just to be sure I heard her right.

Nodding, Sarah smiles widely. "I want that for our family, too."

That's all I need to know. Cupping her's face in my hands, I kiss every tear that falls, only stopping when we notice the fire start to dwindle. I pass her her wine glass before stoking the flames. The quiet night surrounds us, and I feel its peace deep inside.

"So," Sarah says after I have the fire hot again. "What other surprises do you have for me?"

"Well, now it's time for the real bombshell. Are you ready?"

Sarah is already laughing at me. Biting her lip, she nods. So, I reach into the basket and pull out the graham crackers and marshmallows. She leans forward, peering into the basket.

"And chocolate, right? Because the only thing to top this date so far is chocolate."

I reach back into the basket and pull out the chocolate bars. "What is this, my first date ever?"

"Technically?" Sarah says, taking the chocolate from me.

I nod. "Technically, our first date, but between you and me, I'm counting the skid steer as a date."

Chapter 35: Sarah

A part of me can't believe I'm standing in Austin's hardware store, looking at paint for the future nursery he wants to build me, to build us. We haven't even slept together yet, but he's convinced me we want all the same things. He kisses my cheek as he walks by, carrying rollers to put on the shelf.

It is convenient that he owns his own hardware store. Paint is expensive. Construction is expensive. But Austin says he can do most of the work himself, and what he can't, he'll make Connor help him with.

"Pick a colour yet?" Austin asks, giving me another peck on the cheek.

I feel heat on my face and neck as I blush. "How can I pick a colour for a nursery? I mean, there's so much that can happen between now and I don't know when."

He stops and looks me in the eyes. "I'm ready when you are, Sarah. If you want, I can leave Mike in charge, and we can go work on adding to our family right now."

I try to look shocked and offended, but I can't stop laughing. Austin's smile is devious, but he leans in to whisper in my ear. "I hope you know I mean that. I love you."

"I love you," I say as he rubs his nose along the shell of my ear, giving me goosebumps. My heart and mind are racing, competing for top place. My pulse quickens as Austin steps closer, planting soft kisses on my ear and moving to my neck.

Afraid he'll get carried away and completely embarrass me, I shrug my shoulders, nudging him off my neck. "And I believe you."

"As long as you know," he says, kissing me again. Austin walks to the totes he's working out of, grabbing another handful of paint supplies. "How about dinner? What are we cooking?"

"Good question. I should stop by the store."

"We could get some charcoal, a couple of steaks, sit outside under the stars." He sets the last of the brushes in his hands on the shelf and walks back to me. With his hands gently rubbing my arms, his eyes study me. "What do you say? The girls are at a friend's house, so it's just the two of us."

"Sounds nice. I-" A buzzing stops me mid-sentence.

Pulling his phone out, Austin takes a step back. "It's Connor. Give me a minute."

When I nod, he takes another step back. I return to looking at the colour swatches. I'm trying to decide if I want to wait to pick a colour or go with something neutral that I can decorate accordingly, but the sound of Austin's voice pulls at my thoughts. Something is wrong.

"No, I'll be right there." Austin ends the call and turns to me. "Dad had a stroke."

"What? Is he- where is he?" I stammer helplessly.

"In the hospital in Barrie." Standing still, Austin appears in shock.

I set the swatches on the paint counter and wrap my arms around him. For a moment, he simply rests his head on mine. Then he springs into action.

"Mike!" he calls to the back of the store. Before the man can make it to where we are, Austin is pulling his keys out. "I need you and Eric to close up."

As soon as Mike nods in acknowledgement, Austin grabs my hand. We're walking to his truck, and I notice his hands are shaking.

"How about I drive," I say, stopping before he can open the passenger side door. I hold my hand out for his keys.

Austin hesitates but passes them to me. I'm not used to driving such a big vehicle, but I try not to make it obvious. My hands are shaking too, but not like Austin's. He's already lost so much. My heart aches for him. Right now, all I can do is drive. When we're on the highway, I reach for Austin's hand. He gently strokes my wrist with his thumb, not saying a word.

At the hospital, I offer to park the truck and come find him. Austin simply shakes his head, no. So, I do my best to get the wheels in between the lines quickly. Every step feels weighted, like we can't get there fast enough. Time drags on, but in reality, it is probably only a few minutes between the time we walk in, and finding the room number Cal is in. When we find him, he is pale and asleep and attached to a bunch of wires.

My heart can't handle seeing all the Moore men so distraught at once. William and Connor are stoic, but I know William well enough to see through his demeanor. Noah is the worst. His normally irreverent, carefree attitude is nowhere to be found. He stands on the opposite side of Cal's bed from William and Connor, his eyes downcast and his shoulders curled in. Ida sits beside him, holding Cal's hand. Somehow, she seems the calmest, though she is clearly heartbroken.

At first, I hang back, unsure of my place as Austin walks up to his dad. Then William grabs my hand and pulls me forward to stand in front of him, next to Austin. With one hand on my shoulder, his thumb gently rubs at my muscles, and I'm suddenly aware of how tense I am. Unfortunately, seeing Cal hooked up to all these machines, and so pale, only makes things worse.

Other than William holding me in place, the only comfort I find is in the steady beat of the heart monitor hooked up to Cal. It sounds strong, and I hope and pray that he pulls through.

"What happened?" Austin asks, looking to Connor.

Unfolding his arms, Connor opens his mouth to respond, but is interrupted by the door behind him flying open. Charlie sucks in a gasp as she rushes forward, her eyes already red with tears. William's comforting touch is gone in an instant. He reaches Charlie before she collides with Cal's bed, and holds her steady in his arms as she sobs.

Stepping away from the bed, Austin's hand finds mine, lacing our fingers together. We all wait for Charlie. Not that fighting to be heard over her is a problem for Connor, but it's as if all the brothers are letting her express the emotion they hold just below the surface. Austin tugs me closer, and I put my arm around his waist, wishing I could do more for all of them.

Chapter 36: Austin

I watch the heart monitor ticking off the beats as my dad lies motionless. Charlie's tears fill up the space in between. I might fall over if it weren't for Sarah holding me. We've all lost people this way. Our little brother and Charlie's husband, Zach, our mom, my wife. Visions of Jennifer's final moments flip through my mind, and I pull Sarah closer.

For the very first time, a fear over mine and Sarah's plans gnaws at me. *What if it happens to her? How would I survive?*

But I learned a long time ago that I can't live in fear and grief. That's how I missed so much of Lily and Mari's early years. I refuse to live that way now, especially with Sarah. I run my fingers up and down her arm, needing to feel her soft skin.

Connor clears his throat. It's subtle, but when I look over, his eyes narrow on me. His gaze briefly shifts to Sarah and back up. I want to smile, but I can't. My lips twitch, trying to show how I feel, but they're pulled down by the reality of where we are. It's enough for my big brother, though. He gives me a nod before folding his arms across his chest again.

"Charlie, he's going to be okay," he says in the same gruff tone he'd use to tell a waiter his order at a restaurant.

She looks up from William's protective embrace. "Are you sure?"

Connor takes a deep breath. "Yes, thanks to Ida."

All eyes drift to her, but she doesn't respond. Ida watches my dad closer than any of us.

"They were working on a puzzle," Connor continues. "She saw his face start to droop. Dad, of course, said he was fine, but she called me to be sure. I directed an ambulance to her house, and they gave him blood thinners en route. He has a shot at full recovery."

"Thank you, Ida," I say.

She wipes away a tear when she looks up. "Thank Connor, too. I wasn't really sure what was happening. I was just worried. He knew exactly what to do."

Charlie bursts from William's arms and runs around to hug Ida. "Thank you!"

Ida pats her arm in response, still holding my sleeping Dad's hand. As relief settles, I can feel myself begin to relax.

Dad will be okay.

Connor leans over Sarah to whisper in my ear. "You know what this means, right?"

I nod. "We'll have time to convince him of that."

"Of what?" Sarah asks softly.

"He won't be able to stay on his own for a while," Connor tells her. "If Ida hadn't been with him, he could have been alone like that for days."

"We'll figure it out," I say. "He's always welcome with us."

"Speaking of us," Ida says, a bit of her humor shining through the tension in the room. "Is there something you two want to share with everyone?"

Looking down at Sarah, her cheeks turn red instantly. I finally find that smile I was looking for earlier. "Since you ask, Ida. Sarah finally convinced me to go out with her."

Connor scoffs. "Chicken."

"Fine," I say, giving him a well-deserved dirty look. "I finally convinced her to go out with me."

Noah chuckles. "It's about damn time."

"You knew, didn't you?" Connor says, pinning William with a look.

He shrugs, tucking his hands in his pockets. "You know Austin can't get anything done without my help."

"Hopefully, there's at least one thing he can get done without you. This isn't one of those sister wives shows," Noah says, resuming his typical obnoxious grin.

Sarah rolls her face into my chest, groaning. I can't help laughing. I wrap my arms around her. "Yeah, I'll at least try it on my own first. We'll see how it goes."

Connor huffs a laugh, looking amused, smug, but amused. Then Ida clears her throat, drawing all eyes back to her.

"That's one down. Who's next, gentleman?" All three of my brothers shift awkwardly, avoiding her stare. Ida waits, undeterred as she looks at each of them in turn. "Come now, boys. Sarah isn't the only beautiful woman in town."

William's eyes immediately flit to Charlie. Unfortunately, she seems to be the only person in the room who misses it.

"You are the oldest, Connor. How about it?" Ida asks.

"No," my brother answers flatly. "Sarah's taken. You're taken. All hope is lost for me. Noah?"

As my brothers play hot potato with Ida's question, I peer down at Sarah. She's shaking from laughter and a beautiful shade of red. Leaning down, I kiss her forehead. Then I whisper, "I will definitely be trying on my own first, a few things, if I can get away with it."

Her eyes go wide, stilling her laughter. Then she's shaking her head at me.

"I love you, Sarah," I whisper, stealing another kiss.

"I love you, Austin."

"I just heard the L-word. Austin, can you repeat that?" William says, elbowing me. He leans over and says in a low voice "For the love of god, please get Ida's attention back on you and off me."

"The L-word," Connor piles on. "Who said it first?"

The problem is, I honestly can't remember. In a way, I feel like I've been saying it forever. But it really has only been a couple of weeks.

"My money's on Sarah," Noah says.

Slowly turning my head, I glare at him. "And why is that?"

"Because you're a chicken," Connor offers.

I roll my eyes, but it doesn't matter. The fact is, I am in love, and at the moment, knowing that Dad will be okay and Sarah is safe in my arms is enough. Thoughts of my girls tug at my heart, but I know they're safe and sound, too. My world is right side up. It took a tornado to get me there, but it was worth it.

Chapter 37: Austin

Driving back and forth to the hospital in Barrie has taken a toll on my time with Sarah, but Dad seems to be doing really well, all things considered. As I pull in Sarah's driveway, I'm grateful all over again for Ida. Not only did she save my dad's life, but she also offered to take my twins back to the shop with her this afternoon, giving me an extra hour with Sarah.

William and Noah are picking them up from there for some twin-time. I guess it's good that my girls have their uncles to look up to, but sometimes it's hard to tell who the more mature twins are. Either way, an evening of Nerf battles means I'm alone with the woman I love.

Picking up the rose bush out of the passenger seat, I walk up to Sarah's front door and knock. Cut roses may be the more traditional choice, but I know my gardener would rather have this lopsided bush, with one bloom hanging on for dear life.

"Oh, it's beautiful," Sarah says, taking the plant and pushing past me into her garden. "I know just the spot for it, too."

I tuck my hands in my pockets and follow her around to the side of the house where she's built a trellis. Sarah kneels and begins working the rose bush free from its pot. Making myself useful, I walk over to the lean-to and find the trowel.

"Thank you," she says, taking the shovel and digging into the dirt.

I could be miffed that my girlfriend didn't stop to give me a kiss when she saw me standing at her door with flowers, well, *flower*. On the other hand, I love this about her. Watching her care for things is a miracle of nature. When she's finished patting the rose bush into the dirt, she stands. Pushing up on her toes, she kisses me gently.

"I love you," I say, taking the trowel.

Sarah follows me as I put it away. When I turn around, she tilts her head, smiling at me. "I love you. How is your dad?"

I put my arm around her shoulders as we walk back inside. "He's okay. The doctors say everything looks good. It's just a matter of time."

Sarah nods. "And our girls? Did they do okay seeing him in a hospital bed?"

My heart skips a beat when Sarah says 'our girls'. I don't even know if she realizes she said it that way. She loves them as completely as they love her. I swallow the lump that forms in my throat. "They did well. He was so happy to see them. They chatted away, telling him every single detail he's missed."

"I bet they'll be happy when he comes home."

"They certainly will." I pull Sarah closer right before we walk inside and kiss her cheek. Then I let her go ahead of me into the cottage. "I can't believe how much they've changed this summer. I'm dreading the teen years."

Sarah shakes her head. "They'll be fine. You've done a wonderful job raising them so far."

"Well, I'm looking forward to seeing how they handle being big sisters when the time comes," I say the last part softly, thinking how anxious I am to start our life together.

We haven't really talked about all the specifics yet. Truth be told, Sarah and I went into this all backwards. I knew she desperately wanted to have children long before I knew she wanted to have children with me. We said we loved each other before our first official date. This thing between us grew over the summer like her garden, little by little.

Now, here we are. I look around her cottage, and I see my future, and a little of the present scattered everywhere. My hoodie is hanging on the back of her couch. Mari's favourite graphic novel is sticking out from between the cushions. Tina, the begonia, has found her way home, but to a new window. The picture Lily picked out for Sarah hangs on the wall nearby.

"What are you thinking about?" Sarah asks, pulling the lasagna out of the oven.

"You," I say, meeting her eyes. When she blushes, I walk over and put my arms around her, kissing her cheek. "When in doubt, I'm always thinking of you."

A deep, satisfied sigh comes from the woman in my arms, and I'm so happy I'm the man in her life. I press my lips to her temple.

"Can I help with dinner?" I ask, still holding her close.

Sarah giggles. "You'd have to let me go to do that."

"In that case," I say, spinning her around. Holding Sarah's hips, I lean into her until our lips are touching. "I guess we'll go hungry."

An egg timer for the garlic bread steals my thunder, though. Sarah turns, letting me keep my hands on her. "How about you fix us something to drink, while I set the table."

I kiss the back of her head, mumbling into her hair. "Fine."

Food is the last thing on my mind, but I step back and let her work. It does smell amazing. Not as amazing as her, but I promised myself I wouldn't push her. The thought of making love to Sarah takes up a lot of my time lately, but there are things we would need to decide first. I am ready to start a family with her. There is no doubt in my mind, but it's still a big step, one that I want her to be ready for.

Just a matter of time. I pour us both a glass of wine. Sarah looks over at me with those deep brown eyes, and my heart skips a beat. *Just a matter of time.*

Chapter 38: Sarah

Austin's smile captivates me, and I spill half the cheese on the stove. I have to look away or I'm going to ruin dinner. He makes it hard to concentrate on anything else, though. I feel like we've laid all our cards on the table. We want to start a family together. We want to share this cottage and raise the twins here.
But when does that start exactly?

I don't have a good answer, but I know how Austin makes me feel. There's no reason for us to wait, in my mind. Maybe I'm dragging my feet because I'm still struggling to accept that someone could love me so completely. But there's no doubt in my mind that Austin does.

"Alright. There's wine on the table. Iced tea. Shall I set out the silver?" he asks, with that crooked Moore grin.

Shaking my head, I just laugh. Austin finds the silverware and sets it out. Then he helps me serve our dinner. I know I could spend my whole life this way, working beside him, doing anything. After all the projects we tackled together this summer, I know he's going to support me no matter what.

"So, Sarah, there's a bet going," Austin says as he pulls out my chair at the table.

I huff a laugh because a bet can only mean one thing--the Moore brothers are up to trouble. "Okay. Do I want to know?"

"It's not what you need to know. It's what you already know, and more importantly, which team it applies to."

"Team?" I ask, taking a sip of my wine.

Austin nods, solemnly. "The bet is whether you jump ship

to the Know Moores, or if I get dragged to Another Round of Pi."

"Who wouldn't want more pie?" I ask innocently.

His head hangs. "I was afraid you were going to say that."

"Maybe we can compromise. Start a new team."

Austin lifts his head slowly, a tentative smile on his face. "Ready when you are."

I know he's talking about more than trivia. Austin has said something similar every day this week in one way or another. My heart flutters thinking about how sincere he is about us starting a family.

Maybe he really is just waiting on me to decide I'm ready.

"At trivia too," he says, confirming what I'm already thinking.

But that jogs a memory. "Speaking of trivia. How did you know the answer to that question about seconds?"

"Seconds?" Austin's eyebrows knit together.

"Yeah, you know the one about how many seconds are in a year?"

"Oh." The look on his face makes me wonder if I shouldn't have asked. Austin sets his fork down and leans back, an expression of pain in his eyes. "Jennifer," he says softly.

"I'm sorry. I-"

He shakes his head. "I don't mind talking about her, and I hope you're okay with it when I do. She's the girls' mom. I don't ever want them to forget her."

"Of course I don't mind." I reach for his hand and squeeze his fingers. "Will you tell me the story?"

With a shaky breath, he nods. "Our one year anniversary, she gave me a card that said, 'Happy 31,536,000th anniversary.' I asked her what it meant, and she said that she could remember the second she met me, in a math class freshman year, and so we may as well celebrate all of them. And we did, as many as we had together."

"I'm so sorry," I whisper, holding his hand.

Austin puts his other hand over mine. "Me too."

"Can I ask you something?" My voice wobbles, but I think I

finally know what's holding me back.

Austin nods. "Anything."

"How do you think she'd feel about me, about us?"

I'm surprised by Austin's smile. It's slight but confident.

"She'd be cheering us on. Jennifer would be so happy that I found someone who loves our girls and me."

"Really?" I ask, tears in my eyes.

"Jennifer was so down to earth. Practical in every sense of the word. She's probably smiling on us from heaven right now… Mostly."

He dips his head with the last word, and my heart stops. "Why mostly?"

"She was brilliant, but she couldn't hold a candle to your cooking. I think that might make her kind of jealous." Austin says it all in the most even tone. Then he picks up his fork, takes a bite of lasagna, and winks at me.

"You've been spending too much time with Noah," I say, shaking my head. It's a horrible thing to say, but I laugh anyway. That's life with the Moores.

Austin chuckles. "I still miss her every day, but I want you to know that I'm not going to spend our lives comparing you. You're special, Sarah. I want you to know that. You are so special to me."

Deep down, I know Austin means it with all his heart. I can't imagine my life without him now, without his love. He's a part of me in a way I can't explain.

"Do you want to get married?" The words fall out of my mouth so quickly, I can't stop them. Too late, I throw a hand over my mouth.

Austin freezes, his fork halfway to his mouth. "What?"

"Nothing," I mumble through my fingers.

"Sarah Rossi. Did you just ask me to marry you?"

I close my eyes, feeling my nose wrinkle as I wince. "Maybe."

He lets out a heavy sigh. "Connor will never let me live it down if he hears you asked me."

"We can tell him it was your idea," I offer, peeking with one eye open.

Austin leans across the table, takes my face in one hand, and presses his lips to mine. "I knew you were the one, Sarah. If nothing else proves it. That you're willing to pull one over on Connor seals the deal."

"Really?" I ask, laughing. "That's all it takes?"

"Well, I was planning this big romantic evening. Ring shopping. Down on one knee, but this works. Knowing we want all the same things is enough for me."

"You were really planning to propose?" I ask, watching as Austin resumes eating, like this is just another normal conversation.

He takes a sip of wine, then looks me straight in the eyes. "Yes. There aren't enough ways for me to say how much I love you. That seemed like a good way to show you."

My cheeks flush, because I'm surprised all over again by how deeply Austin loves me. I'm quiet as we finish dinner. I'm thinking about how amazing a man he is. When Austin clears his plate, I offer him dessert.

"Maybe later," he says.

After he refills our wine glasses, he moves to the couch. I follow, snuggling into him. Austin puts his arm around my shoulder, and I savor his warmth. I take another sip of my wine and set it on the coffee table.

Turning to face Austin, I put a hand on his chest. His deep blue eyes study me for a moment before he puts his glass down and pulls me to him. Soft kisses quickly turn into more, and I open my lips to let him in. Austin's arms tighten around my waist, drawing me firmly into his lap. All my muscles go weak as heat shoots through my veins. I have to pull back from his kiss, just to catch my breath.

"Sorry," Austin rasps, laying his head on my shoulder. "I didn't mean to get carried away."

Wiggling until he loosens his hold, I stand on weak knees. Austin's eyes come up to meet mine when I hold out my hand.

A sweet smile plays on his lips as he stands, taking my hand in his. Without a word, I lead him to the bedroom in the home we'll share with our children.

Epilogue

(10 months later)

"Pass me the mascara, please," I say, holding out my hand.

Charlie plucks it from her bag and hands it to me. I can't remember the last time we stood next to each other like this, doing our make-up. Charlie puts another pin in my hair, then tugs at the updo to see if it falls.

"Yup. I think it's good."

"What about you? Up or down?" I ask, looking at her in the mirror.

Flipping her red curls, Charlie shrugs. "No one's going to notice my hair anyway. Why waste the time?"

Except William. He's as in love with Charlie as when we were teenagers. Too bad he doesn't act on it.

"Now, how about a nice deep burgundy?" Charlie pulls a tube of lipstick out of her bag and dabs it on my lips. "Very nice. Austin is going to love seeing you in this

My heart skips a beat at the mention of Austin. I can't wait to see him again. It's only been twenty-four hours since Charlie kidnapped me and the girls, but it feels like much longer.

"Do you like the colour of your dress?" I ask, smoothing out the front of my cream dress covered in lace and beading.

"Green makes me feel a little conspicuous with the red hair, but this pale sage isn't bad. Besides," she says, putting an arm around my shoulders. "I'd wear neon green for you."

"You could have had your pick, you know?"

"Yeah, but Ida wanted to do the shopping. How can I say no to her? You look gorgeous."

I let out a sigh, feeling more than beautiful. Austin makes me feel like a rare jewel. I start to smooth out the cotton dress, and my hand stops on my stomach. I turn to the side, but the flowing lace doesn't reveal a thing.

Charlie catches my eye in the mirror. "Are you ready for this?"

"I've never been more ready. Is everyone here?" I ask, looking away from my reflection.

"Noah and William are setting up. Connor is keeping an eye on the troublemakers, Ida and Cal, and the girls are..."

Lily and Mari come into the bedroom, spinning around so their dresses poof out. The desert rose that Ida picked for them looks amazing. She had so much fun dress shopping.

"Dad says they're ready. Are you ready?"

"Ready," I say, smoothing out Mari's hair. "Go stand right beside the door, and we'll be there in a minute."

The twins twirl their way back out. Moments like these, they seem so young. Then other times, they seem so grown up. Charlie steps in front of me, placing a ring of flowers on my head. The yellow and white crown stands out against my dark hair.

Passing me a bouquet of roses, Charlie asks, "Are you sure about this?"

"Yes," I answer on a breath. "I've never been so sure of anything in my life."

She pulls me into a hug. "I'm so happy for you and Austin. You both deserve this kind of happiness."

Then she loops an arm into mine, and we meet the girls. They lead the way out of our cottage, into the orchard. Chairs line either side of the path between the pear trees. The twins walk side by side, followed by Charlie. I walk last with my arm looped around my dad's elbow, admiring all the people here to celebrate with us.

The Moore brothers are lined up behind Austin in tan

suits just a shade darker than my dress. Noah gives me a saucy wink, while William's smile is distracted by Charlie. Right next to Austin, Connor stands with his hands folded in front of him. He gives a curt nod, which I've come to recognize as his love and acceptance.

When I reach the front, I touch the rose on Austin's lapel that matches my bouquet. "You look nice."

"You look amazing, Sarah," he whispers, pulling me into his arms. "I mean it. You're stunning."

"I may be glowing," I say, softly.

Austin leans back, looking curious. "Glowing may not be the word I'd use, but you are radiant."

"There's a reason for that."

"A reason why you're glowing?" he asks. His blue eyes roam over my features as if searching for an answer, then they shoot to mine. "You mean?"

I nod, feeling my smile stretching across my face. "We don't have to wait for what we want, Austin. It's all right here."

His mouth falls open as he looks down at my stomach, then back into my eyes. With his arms around my waist, Austin lays his head on mine. The bouquet is squished between us when the officiant says, "Dearly beloved…"

About The Author

Andrea Kruz

Andrea Kruz is a mother of three and co-author of the new novel, Rossi's Cottage. As a self-proclaimed romance enthusiast, Andrea reads over 200 romance novels a year. She's a mood reader who loves all types of romance books but has a particular weakness for small town stories. Andrea uses all of her reading and daydreaming experiences to develop captivating and endearing storylines and characters. Like our FMC, Andrea spends time every summer near the Georgian Bay, swimming and boating. Andrea lives with her husband and kids in Eastern Ontario where she keeps her raised bed veggie gardens weed-free-ish.

About The Author

Tabi Lawson

Hailing from the deep South, USA, Tabi is a Georgia native with a passion for crafting stories with heart and a little sarcasm. She has a Bachelor's degree in English with a minor in professional writing from Kennesaw State University, and an MBA from Indiana Wesleyan University. As a former librarian, she had a front row seat to the wide variety of books that people love. Once the desire to apply her unique  voice to fiction hit, Tabi began pursuing a Masters of Fine Art in Creative Writing from Liberty University, which she will complete in Spring 2026. She lives a few miles West of Atlanta with her best friend and husband, Dave, their hound dog, and an eclectic collection of classic cars and trucks that tend to creep into her stories.

Manufactured by Amazon.ca
Bolton, ON